Jack
Frost™

Jack Frost

A novelization
by Jennifer Baker

Based on the screenplay
by Mark Steven Johnson
and Steven Bloom
& Jonathan Roberts

SCHOLASTIC INC.
New York Toronto London Auckland Sydney
Mexico City New Delhi Hong Kong

ISBN 0-590-63983-8

Printed in the U.S.A.

12 11 10 9 8 7 6 5 4 3 2 1   8 9/9 0 1 2 3/0

First Scholastic printing, December 1998

1

Charlie Frost joined the stampede out the main doors of school. Vacation! Hundreds of kids rushed the exit as if the first one out won a gazillion dollars.

"Merry Christmas!" he heard Ms. Joseph, the tiny, red-haired music teacher, calling out behind him. "See ya next year!"

Charlie felt a blast of crisp, cold air as he burst outside. He blinked in the bright sunshine. He took off running, his black, knee-high boots crunching on the hard-packed snow.

"Charlie!"

He whirled around to see Nathan Hess racing after him. Nathan had been in his fourth-grade class the year before. "Hey, Charlie, you wanna watch me try and hack into Pizza Hut's mainframe computers?"

"No. I wanna get home." Charlie shook his head apologetically. "My dad's coming back tonight!" he explained hurriedly. Charlie's dad was the coolest, rockingest, bluesiest musician on either side of the Rocky Mountains. He had been on tour with his band for a whole week. But tonight was their last gig.

Then he was sprinting again, across the school lawn and up a sharp crest — a shortcut, but a steep one. His boots sunk way down into the deep snow with each step he took up the hill, but he kept up his pace.

Until he got to the top of the ridge. What he saw on the other side made him stop in his tracks. Down below in the playground a full-scale battle was taking place. It was World War III fought with snow. Half the kids in the elementary school were huddled in a trench on one side of the snow-covered playground, or crouched behind walls of snow they'd erected. On the other side, up on top of the other high ridge, the big kids — the seventh-graders — were launching a brutal attack. It was a major, spare-no-victims battle. White fire flew.

But the elementary schoolers' snowballs didn't soar with the same force or threat as the ones from the enemy camp.

Charlie spotted his three best buds, Tuck, Spencer, and Dennis, taking cover in the trench behind a thick snow wall. Dennis was busy packing a snowball and handing it to Tuck. Tuck stuck his head and arm up just far enough to let the snowball fly. Spencer cowered behind the other two.

Charlie felt a tug of loyalty. His friends needed him. He loped down the ridge and raced toward them, zigzagging through a barrage of airborne snowballs. He dove for cover behind the trench.

"Charlie!" Dennis greeted him.

"All right! The brain's here," Tuck exclaimed.

"What's up?" Charlie asked.

"We thought we were just in a regular snowball fight," Spencer said. "Until they pulled out the heavy artillery."

Suddenly Charlie saw a massive snow cannonball winging right toward them. He had just enough time to put his arms up in front of his face, before the top half of their battlement was obliterated, showering them with cold, wet snow. They all fell backward.

"What was that?!" Charlie sputtered, brushing off the coat of snow that had been dumped on him. He slowly peeked over the shattered remnants of their fortress. A lump of fear rose in his throat. He gulped. Up on the top of the ridge, the seventh-graders had rigged some kind of gigantic, over-grown slingshot — it looked like a canvas mail sack pulled back against python-sized elastic bands that were tied to two old fence posts they'd anchored in the snow. The weapon was manned by Rory Buck, a huge seventh-grader.

You couldn't miss Rory's hard-core snowboarder gear, even from the other side of the playground — the ultra-baggy camouflage pants and the skull-and-bones T-shirt under his open jacket screamed for attention. On either side of him were his two wanna-bes, Mitch and Pudge, just waiting to do the evil Sir Rory's bidding.

"Eat snow, you little wieners!!" Rory yelled. Mitch and Pudge positioned another cannonball, and Rory pulled back on the canvas, letting his mis-sile fly.

Charlie and his three friends curled up, hands over heads. The giant snow boulder whizzed right by Charlie's head and exploded only inches away.

"Alexander!" a girl's voice called out. It was Natalie, his pretty blond neighbor from across the street. Farther down the trench, she stood and pointed toward the lonely stretch of playground between the two warring sides of the snow battle.

Charlie looked across the playground and tensed up. Natalie's little brother, Alexander, was stranded — right in the line of fire.

Natalie looked around, panicked — until she saw Charlie. "Charlie, you've got to help him!"

"Don't worry," Charlie said right away. "I'll get your brother out."

"Yeah, well, I hope so," Natalie said with urgency. "He's got my Discman!" A snowball walloped her in the arm, and she disappeared behind the snow barricade.

A Discman? "I don't have time for this," Charlie muttered under his breath. But little Alexander was getting pelted by snowballs. "Okay, huddle up," he commanded his friends. "Remember what we learned in history class?"

A split second of silence. "No," Tuck and Spencer mumbled in embarrassed stereo.

"Duh!" Charlie said, shaking his head. "If you want to stop an army, stop the general."

"You're going to take on Rory Buck?!" Tuck asked, awe and fear in his voice.

Charlie reached over and zipped Tuck's puffy maroon parka all the way up to his chin and pulled the earflaps on Tuck's hat all the way down, covering up as much skin as possible. "Tuck, you draw their fire," he instructed. Tuck looked like a stuffed teddy bear, all padded and ready to withstand the grenades of snow.

Before Tuck had a second to protest, Charlie took off toward Alexander. "Good luck, man," Spencer called after him.

He made his way through the battlefields of kids and ventured out onto the no-man's-land of the playground. Iceballs zipped and whizzed around his head. Little Alexander had fallen on the ground. Charlie glanced up toward Rory. The bully was pulling back another snow boulder in the canvas slingshot, aiming right at the defenseless second-grader. Then he saw something and readjusted his aim.

Charlie glanced behind him. Tuck was up on the field now, taking a hit from a snowball. It bounced off his well-stuffed parka. Tuck's grin seemed to say, *Hey, that didn't even hurt*. He took several giant steps farther out onto the battlefield and got hit by another snowball.

Rory followed Tuck's movements and drew back the overgrown slingshot.

Charlie scrambled forward to Alexander. He grabbed the little boy and stood him on his feet. "Are you okay?" he asked. "Run! Run!" he added, without waiting for an answer.

Alexander started moving.

Up on the ridge, Rory got ready to fire his missile. Charlie saw Pudge whack Rory on the arm and point to the fleeing Alexander. The snow boulder misfired, shooting out of the slingshot at a wild angle. Charlie followed its flight through the air. It nailed Barry Williams, a sixth-grader, right in the butt.

Up on the ridge, Rory gestured angrily at Pudge. Then he looked down at the battlefield, where Alexander was racing toward his sister. The next thing Charlie knew, Rory was on his snowboard and jetting down the ridge, heading straight for the defenseless Alexander.

"Run!" Charlie heard Natalie yell. "Run like the wind, Alexander!"

Charlie jumped directly in Rory's top-speed

path. He held his breath as the huge bully came snowboarding toward him.

Rory made a sharp, sideways stop, bombarding Charlie with a spray of snow. "Well, well, well," he sneered. "Little Charlie Frost. Hanging with the second-graders now?" He bent down and scooped up a big pawful of snow. "Can you say 'brain-freeze'?" He glanced over his shoulder at Pudge and Mitch up on the ridge.

Charlie acted with lightning speed. He gathered up snow in both hands and packed it into a dense ball. As Rory turned back to him, Charlie let his snowball fly. It smacked Rory hard in the face. "Brainfreeze!" Charlie yelled triumphantly.

Rory fell back on the slippery ground.

Charlie wiped the leftover snow from his mittens and began walking away.

"This isn't the end of it, Frost!" Rory yelled after him. He tried to get up, but his snowboard slid out from under him again. Up on Bad Boy Ridge, even his friends were laughing at him.

"Shut up!" Rory roared. Charlie was laughing at him, too. Rory worked furiously to loosen his boots from his snowboard. He finally made it to his feet, but the battle was over. And it was clear who had won. He tucked his snowboard under his arm and beat a retreat up the hill.

A victory whoop went up from Charlie's side. Charlie walked back to the cheering troops and sought out Alexander and Natalie. Natalie had her brother by one hand and her Discman in the other hand.

"Are you okay?" Charlie asked the little boy.

"Yeah," Alexander said, looking up at Charlie like he was a hero.

"You were amazing, Charlie," Natalie added. "Thanks."

Charlie grinned. "No problem. See ya later."

"See ya at hockey practice," Natalie said.

And Charlie took off at top speed for home.

2

Charlie raced through his little Colorado town. He didn't slow down until he'd made it up his walkway and burst through the front door of his yellow-shuttered house. His scrappy white terrier, Chester, barked and slipped in behind him before the door slammed shut.

Charlie raced into the kitchen. A pair of legs in blue jeans stuck out from under the sink. "Dad?" he said eagerly.

But Gabby Frost, her shoulder-length blond hair tied up in a ponytail, slid out from under the cabinetry and sat up, a wrench in her hand. Charlie felt a beat of disappointment. Mom.

His mother smiled at him. "Charlie, it's a long drive from Denver. You know he won't be back until late." She stood up, put the wrench down on the kitchen counter, and wiped her hands on the legs of her jeans. "I don't get it. Sometimes it leaks, sometimes it doesn't," she said.

"Dad'll fix it," Charlie assured her.

Gabby gave a little sigh. "He's been saying that since you were in kindergarten." His mother stooped back down and positioned a large metal bucket under the leaky drainpipe. Charlie could hear the hollow *ping, ping* of water hitting the bucket bottom. Gabby stood up again. "So . . ."

"So . . ." Charlie echoed. His mother was looking at him as if he'd forgotten something.

"So . . . *not* turning over a report card right away is a bad sign."

Oh. That. Charlie dug into the inside pocket of his jacket. The envelope with his report card was crumpled and slightly damp. He held it out to her.

As she took it, he grabbed his hockey stick and a puck from the mudroom off the kitchen. He heard his mother give a low whistle. Charlie had aced it — all A's. "You may have your father's looks, but you get your brains from me."

Good, Charlie thought as he pushed out the back door. He went around to the front and

11

smacked the puck into the target painted on the front of the garage door. The puck gave a satisfying thump, even if it missed the center of the target. Charlie aimed again.

Every few minutes he glanced down the street to see if his dad was coming.

Jack Frost could almost imagine the headlines: Discovered in Denver over Dumplings! That's what they'd be saying when his band hit the big time. And this dude in front of him, hotshot record exec, John Kaplan, was just about to make that happen.

In a back booth of Denver's Hunan Palace, far from his sleepy Medford, Colorado, hometown, John was explaining that he'd been following the Jack Frost Band from gig to gig all week — and was ready to sign them up to a juicy recording contract. It was everything Jack had been struggling for all these years.

Kaplan stabbed the air with his chopstick to make his point. "I think if we make a tape that kicks butt, I can push it through."

All right! Jack's pulse beat out an excited drumroll. The band would make the tape, Kaplan would play it for the big boys at the record company —

and snap! The Jack Frost Band had it made in the shade. Fame, acclaim, and enough dough to buy his family a new house, a car that actually started — and the newest, best, top-of-the-line hockey skates and gear for Charlie. Heck, Charlie's own private rink, if he wanted it.

The Jack Frost Band — an overnight sensation that had taken, oh, only about a decade! Their time was now. All they needed to do was make one more tape.

Charlie was dreaming. Something about Mom and Dad and a tube of Chap Stick.

"Listen, I lost my lip balm a couple of blocks away. I was wondering, could I borrow some of yours?" his father was saying. Then Charlie heard some sappy, kissy noises. He started to get the feeling he wasn't dreaming. He struggled to open his eyes.

His parents' footsteps got closer. "Shh," his mother said. "He tried to wait up."

"Wow. I've only been gone a week," his father whispered.

"That feels like forever when you're eleven," Gabby replied.

Charlie stirred under his favorite Denver Broncos blanket. He half opened one eye. He was on the living room sofa. The Christmas tree twinkled with colorful lights, a gauzy angel perched at the top. He let his eyes close again.

"Charlie. Charlie-boy. The old man's home," his father crooned softly. Charlie felt Dad plant a gentle kiss on his head.

"Jack, maybe we should let him sleep," his mother said.

But Charlie was waking up. "He has all vacation to sleep!" his father pronounced.

"Dad? Oh, man, I musta fell asleep," Charlie said.

"That's okay, Charlie-boy, you go back to sleep. Oh, just a little weather update for you. It's snowing!" his father said, gleefully.

Snowing? Charlie was wide-awake now. "Yea!" He bolted up and pulled back the curtain behind the sofa. Big, fat, soft flakes were falling fast and thick. He grinned. This was going to be the whitest Christmas ever.

And his whole family was together to enjoy it.

3

A few minutes later, Charlie was out on the front lawn, the snowflakes settling on his face and eyelashes. He'd pulled his boots and his parka over his pajamas, and he was busy rolling the middle ball of a snowman.

His father had positioned the big bottom ball, and was working on the top one now.

"Dad, don't make him a fathead," Charlie instructed.

"It's not a fathead!" Jack protested. "He's just smart. He needs a huge cranium to hold his brain."

"A smart snowman. Yeah, right, Dad." Charlie laughed. Chester nipped friskily at his heels.

"Woof, woof," his father barked playfully at Chester.

Chester growled. Not a friendly sound.

Dad took a step backward. "Chester's still not much of a blues fan," he commented.

"Relax, Dad," Charlie reassured him. "Sometimes he just doesn't recognize you."

His father got a sad look in his eye. "Really?" he asked softly.

Oops. Charlie hadn't meant to make the old man feel bad. But Dad *was* away kind of a lot. And it wasn't Chester's fault. Charlie loaded his boulder onto the base. His father popped the head on.

"Okay . . . eyes," Charlie said.

Jack grabbed two stones from the part of the driveway Gabby had shoveled earlier in the day. "Close in? Far apart?" he asked. "Third eye here?"

"No, he's not an alien!" Charlie protested, laughing. "He's human. Right . . . there!" He waited until his dad had gotten the eyes the right distance apart. "Okay, nose."

His father reached into his pocket and took out the carrot stick they'd snagged from the fridge.

"Okay, mouth time," Charlie instructed. He looked at his father's huge, happy grin. He stepped up to Mr. Snowman and swiftly drew the same smile with his thumb. "Arms," he said.

He and his father each scouted for the right shaped branches and jammed them in on either side of the middle ball. Dad pulled three buttons out of his pocket and held them out. Charlie slapped them down the snowman's front. He stepped back to examine their handiwork. Something was missing. "Hmm . . . scarf," he said.

His father took off his burgundy scarf with the gray stripes. He wrapped it around the snowman's fat neck. "Satisfied?" he asked.

"Gloves and hat," Charlie demanded.

His father threw his hands up in mock surrender. "You're tough. You are tough!" But he put his red mittens and his famous porkpie hat on the snowman.

"Kinda looks like you, Dad," Charlie joked.

"Only cuter," his mom chimed in with a laugh. Charlie turned to see her standing on the front step.

"Oh, really?" Jack said with mock irritation. He scooped up some snow, gave it a few packs, and sent it flying. It missed her.

"Aghh! Okay, you asked for it," Gabby said.

She hopped off the step and onto the lawn, packing her own snowball and flinging it at Jack. A spirited Frost family snowball fight had begun!

*   *   *

Later, Jack tucked Charlie into bed. "Nice work on that snowman, dude," he complimented his son.

"Yeah, that was fun," Charlie said. He slid deep under the covers. It felt nice to be in his comfortable room, surrounded by his posters — one of dad's band, another of his hockey star idol, Wayne Gretzky — and his closets that overflowed with equipment for just about any sport you could name — hockey, hoops, soccer. . . .

He yawned and started to turn over. Then he stopped. "Dad? Did you bring me anything?"

His father looked as if he'd been thrown a curveball. He fished around in his pockets. Charlie felt disappointed.

"Oh, sure," his father bluffed. "Most musicians' kids get broken guitar picks, or drink coasters, or a box of those little swords they stick olives on," he said. "But that doesn't cut it with me." He pulled a silver harmonica out of a pocket.

"One of your harmonicas?" Charlie said harshly.

"Hey. It's not just one of my harmonicas. This harp has special powers."

"Yeah, right," Charlie said.

"Really," Dad insisted. "An old blues man

named . . . named . . ." He glanced at the poster of Wayne Gretzky. ". . . Sonny Boy Wayne gave this to me. Any time you need me, no matter where I am, you just play on this harp. I'll hear you." He pressed the harmonica into Charlie's hand.

Charlie examined it. A regular harmonica, the shine dulled a bit from wear. "You just made that up," he stated. But he folded his hand around the harmonica and clutched it tightly.

His father bent down and kissed him on the cheek. "Good night, Charlie-boy." He began to walk toward the door.

"Dad — I'm playing hockey tomorrow. Can you come?" Charlie held his breath for the answer. His father hadn't made it to a game yet.

"Actually, buddy, me and the guys have to record some songs tomorrow. . . ."

Charlie felt a wave of disappointment. "My game's not till four o'clock. It's against our archrivals, the Devils."

"You're eleven years old. You already have an archrival?" his father asked, surprised.

"Yep," Charlie said proudly.

"What did you say . . . four o'clock? You know what? I'm there," Jack assured him.

"Really?" Charlie felt hope.

"I promise," his father said.

All right! Charlie thought triumphantly as his father headed for the door and reached for the light switch. On a whim, Charlie brought the harmonica to his lips and blew a few notes.

His father turned back toward him. "Yeesss?" he singsonged.

"Just testing it," Charlie told him.

"Good night, Charlie." Dad turned off his light.

Outside, on the front lawn, the solitary snowman stood guard.

4

Charlie whacked a tennis ball with his hockey stick and sent it shooting down the driveway. Mac, Jack Frost's best friend and roly-poly keyboard player, was helping Gabby hang a string of red-and-green Christmas lights over the front door. Mac's funky old Cadillac sat at the curb.

"Frost with the puck!" Charlie announced to himself. "He crosses the blue line on a breakaway. He shoots —" Charlie slammed the ball at the goal on the garage door. Darn! Wide by at least five feet. "Ohhh! Hit the post," he said.

"Who taught you to shoot like that?" his father asked him, coming over toward the driveway.

"Coach Gronic," Charlie answered.

"Dicky Gronic?" Jack said. "He doesn't know a puck from a potato."

Charlie laughed. "No, Dicky's brother Sid is the coach."

"Oh, Sid Gronic is one of the great hockey minds of the century," his father said sarcastically. He took the hockey stick out of Charlie's hands, gracefully maneuvered the ball into place, and took a shot. The ball slammed right into the center of the target.

"He shoots! He scores!" Jack Frost gave a play-by-play. "Yes, baby!"

Charlie felt a swell of admiration. "Wow! What the heck was that?" Charlie asked him.

"That, my friend, is the J-shot," Dad said.

"You've got to teach it to me." With a shot like that, Charlie knew he couldn't be stopped.

"I don't know, Charlie. It's top secret," his father said teasingly.

"It is not, Dad. C'mon!" Charlie protested.

"Charlie, Dad's gotta go," his mother called from the front step. "It's eleven-thirty. He's already late." Not that Dad was ever on time.

His father looked over at his mother. "It takes about two seconds," he said to her. He turned back to Charlie. "It's all about relaxation."

"What do you mean?" Charlie asked.

Dad handed the hockey stick back to Charlie. He came up behind him and put his arms parallel to Charlie's on the stick. Meanwhile, Mac was getting into his big, old car. "Just relax your forearms," Dad instructed. He shook the stick gently to loosen up Charlie's muscles. "Good! Now the key is the wrists."

"Frost!" Mac called from the driver's seat of the Caddy.

"Jack!" Gabby seconded.

Jack sighed and let go of the hockey stick. "Okay, I gotta go. I'll show you later." He headed for Mac's car.

"But, Dad . . ." Charlie protested.

His father looked over his shoulder at him. "What'd you call me? Buttdad?"

Not funny. At least not very. "But, Dad," Charlie said, more weakly the second time.

"Buttdad? Sid Gronic teach you that kind of language?" his father asked. He climbed into the passenger seat and shut the door. The Cadillac pulled away from the curb.

Charlie watched it disappear down the street.

*   *   *

Crash! Dennis got smashed right into the glass at the side of the hockey rink by Rory's sidekick Pudge.

"Why couldn't I grow up in Hawaii?" Charlie heard Dennis lament, as he skated over at lightning speed to rescue the puck.

Charlie got his stick on it and let it fly. It flew. Way wide. Up into the stands. He followed it with his eyes. He cringed as it sailed toward a spectator, knocking the baseball cap right off his head. Oops.

But Charlie barely had time to worry about it. Suddenly he was getting bodychecked, and — oof! The wind went right out of him as he got slammed into the boards.

"Nice shot . . . if you're golfing." Rory Buck! Charlie hadn't even seen Rory coming.

Charlie struggled to get his wind, sucking in a wheezy gulp of air. Ooooh! Ow! Rory nailed him with a big, painful elbow to his ear. "Nobody brainfreezes Rory Buck."

The scoreboard bore grim news. Mountaineers: 0, Devils: 3. The scorekeeper just shook her head.

Coach Gronic got his team into a huddle. "I know you're just kids," he said, "and we're really here to teach you fair play and sportsmanship and all that, but . . . I . . . am . . . so tired of looking up and seeing it's three to zero." Coach Gronic's face was beet red. "Again, and again, and again. . . ."

"Lighten up, Dad," Tuck said.

"Sorry, but history is made by winners!" Coach Gronic thundered. "Conquerors! Barbarians!" His big, loose cheeks shook. His chins trembled — all of them. "So get out there and wipe the ice with their filthy butts!!"

Natalie gave Charlie a private nudge and made a couple of circles around her ear with her index finger.

Charlie nodded in agreement. Tuck's dad had definitely lost it.

But at least Tuck's dad was *here*. As he skated back out onto the ice, Charlie scanned the stands. Again. Mom was up in the bleachers. Alone. He forced a smile at her, but he felt as deflated as a popped balloon. Dad had promised. Again. And broken his promise. Again.

"Come on, Dennis!" Dennis's dad yelled. Charlie sagged a little.

"Come on, Spencer!" both of Spencer's parents

called from the front row. Charlie sagged a little more.

"You can do it, Natalie!" yelled Natalie's father, along with Alexander.

"Come on, Charlie!" his mom yelled. Charlie let out a sigh.

"Hey, sweetheart, miss me?" Charlie heard a mean voice say. He looked over to see Rory eyeing him like a T-rex might eye his prey. Then his attention shifted as the ref dropped the puck for the face-off. The Devils got it.

And Rory got Charlie. He charged straight into him and flattened him onto the ice.

Mountaineers: 0, Devils: 5. The news just kept getting worse. Charlie stared at the scoreboard as if giving it the evil eye would magically change the score. The scorekeeper put away a whole Kit Kat bar in a couple of bites, looking bored.

Suddenly, Rory shoved Charlie. Charlie tripped over his own skate blade and went flying. He flailed his body in midair, sailing crazily. Hands out to break his fall, he kept skidding across the slick, cold ice. Going, going . . . smack into Dennis. Who, caught unaware, slid right into Tuck. The domino effect. One down, the next one down, all of them down — and they slid right into the net.

Charlie heard a hoarse guffaw and looked up to see the old goalkeeper laughing at them. And Mom still up in the bleachers by herself.

Next period, no better. Charlie found himself sandwiched by Mitch and Pudge. Wow, was he gonna need a hot bath for his bruised muscles tonight. But what hurt even more was looking up at Mom and seeing that Dad wasn't with her. And the Devils had six points now. To the Mountaineers' big, round, hollow, empty nothing.

And then seven points. To zip. And no Dad. Eight points. Nada. Zip. Dad unaccounted for. Coach Gronic was getting angrier and redder. By the final seconds of the game he was almost purple in the face. Zero. The Mountaineers were major zeros. Maybe it was just as well that Dad couldn't be bothered to witness this defeat. Charlie felt a surge of anger. And at that same moment, he saw it — the puck — loose on the ice.

Channeling every ounce of that anger into his skating, he zoomed forward and got his stick on the puck before anyone else. Maybe the Mountaineers couldn't win, but they didn't have to go down in complete, total, zero-sucking defeat. Charlie brought his arms back. And forward again and . . . *boom!* He smacked the puck.

But he could see the result of his shot even before it missed the net. Ten feet wide of his goal. He flinched at the sharp, nasal sting of the scorekeeper's buzzer. Game. And definitely not theirs.

Rory high-fived Mitch and Pudge on the other side of the rink. Their victory noises echoed through the stadium. Animals in triumph. Top of the food chain. Hear us roar.

Charlie flashed them a look of disgust and skated over to the bench. He couldn't remember *ever* feeling this low.

5

Jack Frost let out the final, haunting note on his harmonica. It hung in the studio air, as bittersweet and delicious as a rich, dark chocolate bar.

Over in the sound booth, John Kaplan, big kahuna record man with the long sideburns, grinned. "That was pure smoke, guys. You want to break? Maybe order some supper?"

Frost's eyes shot to the clock behind John Kaplan. Supper? Oh, baby, it was 6:30. Charlie! The hockey game! He felt his pulse take off like a 747 as he sprinted for the door. The frigid evening air stung him like a reprimand. How had he let the entire afternoon slip away in the studio without even realizing it? How had he gotten so wrapped up in his music that he hadn't even looked at the clock? Or remembered Charlie's game?

Mac raced after him to give him a lift in the Caddy. But Frost couldn't have gotten home fast enough if Mac had a race car.

Jack felt horrible as he headed nervously up his walkway. He noticed that Gabby had shoveled it. Even though he'd said he'd do it. Bad sign.

Suddenly, something sprung out of the hedges at him. He felt a beat of fright. *Grrrr.* Oh. Chester. "How bad is it in there, Chester?"

The dog gave another low, menacing growl. "That bad, huh?" Frost asked. He sighed. Maybe Gab and Charlie would understand that today was different. That this tape the band had made might change everything. Change their lives — Frost's and Gabby's and Charlie's.

Then again, maybe they'd just see that he'd messed up again. Said he'd be there for Charlie. Said he'd be part of the family. And completely forgotten. They'd be right.

He let himself into the house, his hand trembling slightly as he worked his key. He found Gabby in the kitchen. The dirty dinner dishes were stacked in the sink. Except for Jack's. His place was still set at the round kitchen table. Untouched. Gabby was sitting at her place. She barely moved when he walked in. Except to look up at him, her pretty face tight. "You promised him, didn't you?"

"I —" Jack scrambled for a decent excuse.

"Why did you go and do that, Jack?"

Because he'd really meant it. At the time.

"How many times have I told you, if you're not going to show up, don't *say* you're going to show up."

She was right of course. But he'd had every intention of showing up.

"You know how I knew you promised him? He kept looking up at me in the stands. After about, I don't know, the fortieth time, I realized he expected you to be there."

Frost had a flash of Charlie down on the ice, looking up into the bleachers, his face colored by disappointment. Frost felt a tidal wave of guilt.

"Jack, I don't care if you get too busy or you flake out on *me*," Gabby said. "Well, I care," she corrected herself. "But I chose it. I married you. I'll deal with it. But he didn't choose this, Jack."

Frost inhaled. What could he say? Gabby was one hundred percent right.

"One of these days Charlie's gonna score his first goal, and you won't see it. Just like you never saw him with the chicken pox or the time he jammed the Fig Newtons into the slide projector. Those things only happen once and they're gone."

Frost was deeply sorry. He remembered what it was like to be out there on the ice, the final seconds of the game lit up on the score clock, your stick on the puck, your teammates yelling for you, the fans yelling for you. And your family — calling out your name because the whole game depended on you. Frost remembered the rush of sending that puck flying across the ice. Sort of like the rush of being in the recording studio and getting a song exactly right. It was the most important thing in the world. "Gabby . . ." Frost opened his mouth to apologize.

"Don't, Jack." She stopped him before he'd started. "You've said enough."

There really *wasn't* much to say, and Frost knew it. He'd let Charlie down, and it had hardly been the first time. He felt a hollow ache in the pit of his stomach.

"How d'ja do?"

From inside the tent he'd made from his blanket, Charlie heard his father's voice. He went tight with anger, squeezing the flashlight he held as if he were trying to crush it. The flashlight cast a warm, dim glow inside the tent, but it didn't feel cozy in there the way it usually did. Charlie was too angry. What did Dad care how the game had gone? It was just kids' stuff. Not important enough to bother with.

"We got slaughtered. Eight–zip."

"Oh, Charlie, I'm sorry I didn't make it. Did you use the J-shot?"

Hel-lo. How was he supposed to do that? "You haven't taught it to me yet," Charlie reminded him.

"Right," his father said with a sigh. "Look, Charlie, I need to talk to you about something that's kind of important."

"Okay," Charlie said. But he didn't really feel like it was okay. He just felt like he was going to have to listen to some excuse. And he'd heard them all before. Weren't grown-ups supposed to be the responsible ones? Usually it was the kids making excuses to their parents. Something was wrong with this picture. Charlie steeled himself for his dad's words.

"Charlie-boy . . ." he said imploringly. But

Charlie wasn't going to let it get to him. "I'm chasing a dream I've had since I was a kid," his father said. "Like you want to be the next Wayne Gretzky, I wanted to be —"

"Sonny Boy Wayne?" Charlie cut in, thinking about Dad's made-up blues musician. Dad had been scrambling for an excuse then, and he was doing the same thing now. But Dad didn't seem to catch Charlie's meaning.

"Oh, yeah . . . Yeah! Sonny Boy Wayne. And you know, if you work hard enough and stay true to yourself, you'll reach your goal. And I might finally be reaching mine."

"That's good, Dad," Charlie said. Well, he *did* want his father to get what he wanted. To be a famous musician. To have people know how good he was. Charlie wanted that, too. Still . . .

"Yes, it is good," his father said, "but the bad thing is, if you don't watch out, you can turn into kind of a selfish jerk who sometimes screws up. Y'see?"

Yeah. Charlie did see. Very clearly. Unfortunately. And it really hurt. "So . . . are all musicians selfish jerks?" he asked his father.

"No. . . . Yes, they are. . . ." his father corrected himself.

Charlie felt a teeny, tiny giggle escape his lips, despite how mad he was.

"But my point is . . ." his father went on. "Tell you what. Why don't we spend Christmas in the mountains? We'll go to the cabin at Pine Top."

Pine Top. The place Charlie and his parents liked to go to get away, just the three of them. Lots of running around in the snow. Skating on the pond. Roaring fires in the fireplace. Big meals. Nothing they had to do. Nowhere they had to go.

"No band," Dad was saying. "No phones. No TV. Just us. Having a real vacation. What do you say, Charlie-boy?"

"Will you teach me the J-shot?"

"I'll teach you the J-shot. Honest."

Charlie had a flash of whipping the hockey puck past Rory and his thugs and smashing it into the goal. It would be cool to know the J-shot. He felt his grasp on the flashlight loosen. Just a little. Who could say no to a Christmas at Pine Top?

6

Charlie dragged his duffel bag down the hall toward the front door. He strained at the canvas strap. His parents, at the open door with an assortment of suitcases and overnight bags, looked up at him.

"What's in there, a body?" his father asked.

Charlie giggled. "Walkman, Game Boy, batteries, food."

"Charlie, it's only three days," Dad said.

Out the open door, Charlie saw the snow still coming down heavily. "We could get snowed in for months," he said. He dragged his duffel bag down the rest of the hallway.

He gave a little start as the phone on the hall table rang shrilly. Charlie glanced over at his parents, wedged in the doorway with all the bags. He let go of his own duffel and grabbed the phone on the third ring.

"Hello, Frost residence," he said.

"Hello, Jack Frost, please," said a man's voice. "This is John Kaplan."

Charlie covered the receiver with one hand. "Dad, it's for you. John Kaplan?" Charlie hoped his dad wouldn't take the call. What could be so important on Christmas Eve day?

But Dad dropped his bags like hot potatoes and lunged for the phone. "Hello?"

Charlie wanted to stick around and spy on Dad's end of the conversation, but his mother came over and started tugging on his duffel bag. "C'mon," she said quietly. "Let's get the car loaded up so we're ready to leave when your father gets off the phone."

They had the back of the Jeep half packed when Dad burst out of the house, grinning like he'd hit the jackpot in the zillion-dollar lottery. He gave the snowman on the lawn a pat on the butt as he rushed past it. "They loved our tape!" he gushed to Gabby and Charlie. "They're signing us to a contract!"

"All right!" Charlie said. This was what Dad

was talking about the night before. About working toward a dream — and getting there. Sonny Boy Wayne and all that. But this time it was real!

"Oh, Jack, I'm so happy for you," Gabby said, smiling broadly.

Jack Frost hugged his wife and then folded Charlie into his arms, too. "Yeah! Well, listen to this — Asylum's head guy wants us to come to his chalet in Aspen. We'll sign the contract and then play for his crazed Hollywood Christmas bash."

Gabby took an abrupt step away from Jack. "When?" she asked.

"Well . . . tomorrow."

Tomorrow? Did that mean they were going to some fancy Christmas party in Aspen instead of to Pine Top? Well, it wouldn't be as quiet, but it sounded kind of fun and wild.

Charlie's mother didn't seem pleased, however.

"Tomorrow's Christmas, Jack," she said in a soft, tight voice.

"Of course!" Dad said. "It's just that this guy . . . he's the head guy! He wants us to play for him. That's huge. So, can we maybe just figure this out?"

"What time is the party?" Mom sounded really annoyed now.

"Like, seven. So the band would ride up today and if I can get out of there tomorrow by eight-fifteen, eight-twenty . . ."

Charlie felt as if he'd been smacked across the face. *The band would ride up.* . . . Not Charlie and Mom and Dad and the band. Just the band.

"Jack, that means midnight," his mother was saying. His father was outta here. Gone. Not home until way past his bedtime. He was going to miss every minute of Christmas with Charlie.

But Dad was still doing his it's okay routine. "Eight-thirty, tops!" he said. "If I drive straight through, I could make it back before Santa's official midnight deadline. That's still Christmas! I can do this, honest. Okay?"

Still Christmas. What, for one more second? Why even bother?

"It's not up to me," Charlie's mother said stiffly. "You have to make your own decision."

"C'mon, Gabby, I swear, I'll fill my guitar case with fancy, rich people's desserts. I can do this."

Sure, Dad. You can do this. And we can spend Christmas without you, Charlie thought.

"Well, you should go, then," Gabby said, her voice barely under control.

Dad looked at Charlie. Charlie dropped his gaze to the snow-covered ground. He was afraid that if he looked back at his father, he might start to cry. And he was much too angry to let Dad think he was worth it.

Charlie sat in the backseat of the Jeep with Chester. Dad poked his blond, spiky-haired head in through the driver's window. He gave Gabby a kiss on the cheek. She didn't respond, and Charlie didn't blame her one bit.

"Okay, be safe. I love you, and I'll see you in, like, sixteen hours," Jack Frost said, as if everything were totally okay.

"I love you, too," Gabby said, but she didn't sound very convincing. "Break a leg," she added. In this case, she might have been angry enough to really mean it. Charlie was.

When Dad came around to his side, Charlie was ready. He dug into his parka pocket and pulled out the harmonica Dad had given him the other night. "Here. This is yours." He tried not to let his voice tremble.

"Charlie, that's the harmonica I gave you," his father protested.

Chester let out a long, low growl. Yeah, Charlie knew exactly how Chester felt. "Just take it," he told his father. "I don't want it." Sure. Dad would be there whenever Charlie blew into it. Except when he was in the recording studio. Or out playing a gig. Or rehearsing with his band. Or going to some big shot's big-deal Christmas party. Dad there for him whenever he needed him? Right. And that snowman on the lawn was going to blink and come to life.

"I'll . . . see you later," his father said. Charlie could hear the sadness in Dad's voice, but he wasn't going to let it get to him. No way. It was Dad's own fault if he felt lousy. He *should* feel lousy. The problem was Charlie felt lousy, too.

Mom turned the car key in the ignition. She didn't even wait for the Jeep to warm up. She just floored the gas pedal and took off quickly. Charlie resisted the temptation to look back.

7

Mac's Cadillac was like the ocean liner of cars. Big and comfortable. Normally, Jack liked taking the Caddy on road trips — new places to see, the feeling that a surprise could be waiting right around a curve in the road.

But now, a few hours away from signing his record contract and a giant step toward the biggest dream of his life, Jack was slumped in the passenger seat, miserable. Behind them, Andy's van carried the rest of the band and their equipment.

They passed a road sign: Aspen, 263 miles. Two hundred sixty-three miles on some snowy, twisting, turning mountain roads. That was, let's see . . . at least five hours. . . . Which meant it was even more than that back to Pine Top and Gabby and Charlie.

No way he'd be at the cabin by midnight. Not that a few hours more or less mattered, anyway. He had walked away with the award for Rotten Dad. But what was he supposed to do? This was his work. This was what he had to do.

"We gotta do this gig," he said to Mac. "It's a huge deal."

"Absolutely," Mac agreed. He stared straight ahead at the slippery road.

"I mean, it's an honor, right? Playing at the guy's house?"

"Oh, it's big," Mac confirmed.

"Big? It's the head honcho."

"Exactly."

Well, thought Jack, at least one person understands. He flicked on the radio. A Christmas melody filled the car. Triangles and bells rang out their holiday message.

"Hey, Mac, remember our very first Christmas gig together?" Jack asked, trying to get into the spirit.

"It was right after you came through London and swept me off my feet," Mac said jokingly.

Back when Jack had been single. Back when he could go anywhere, whenever he wanted, without anything tying him down. It had been . . . lonely. Strange hotels, strange food, too busy moving from concert to concert to really see the places they were traveling to, far away from people you knew and loved. . . .

"Pull over," he ordered Mac. The words popped out of his mouth before he'd even realized what he was saying.

"With pleasure," Mac said. He cracked the first smile of the day.

"If we were good enough for Asylum Records this morning, we're good enough for them tomorrow morning," Frost reasoned.

"Fancy party or no fancy party," Mac agreed, as he signaled to Andy in the van and pulled over onto the shoulder of the road.

"Right. I don't care how big a honcho this head honcho is, some things are just flat-out more important." Now that Jack had started, it felt good to get it off his chest. If they were going to be big stars, they could start acting like big stars. Beginning this second. Jack let himself out of the Caddy. Mac got out his side and they walked toward Andy's van. "What the heck was I thinking?" Jack said.

"Don't be so hard on yourself, Frost. You've been after this dream a long time."

"I know," Jack replied, "but I haven't been that hot of a father along the way. It's time I got my priorities straight. I'm gonna go be with my family." Jack felt a warm breeze of relief. For once he was going to do the right thing.

And then he realized he'd walked right by the van and was trudging back down the shoulder of the road in the direction they'd come from. Without his coat. Or hat. Mac was staring after him, laughing.

Jack whirled around. "What am I doing? It's freezing!"

Mac tossed Jack the keys to the Cadillac and climbed into the van. Jack tromped back to the Caddy in the snow. As he passed the van, he peered in. "Merry Christmas, guys!"

His happiness echoed through the gray Colorado afternoon.

The sky had grown dark. The snow fell in large, moist flakes, swirling in the headlights of the Caddy like flying angels. The road curved and dipped its way through the mountains. Inside, the car was warm. Jack felt more peaceful than he had in a long, long time. "I can't believe it, Charlie-boy," he said softly. "I'm gonna be there."

The snow began to come down harder, collecting on the road like a fleecy, white blanket. It covered the windshield. The wipers pushed at their heavy, wet load and then got bogged down.

Jack rolled his window open. He was hit with a burst of cold air as he reached around in front of him, to grab the wiper. He pulled the wiper up and lifted his foot off the accelerator to slow down. He ran his bare hand along the wiper, stripping off the icy clumps of snow. He let the blade snap back down, sweeping a clean arc on the windshield.

Jack looked out and his heart jumped into his throat. He couldn't even scream. The guardrail at the edge of the road was smack in front of him. The car was gliding toward it. And behind it, the road dropped off into a steep, tree-lined slope.

He slammed his foot down on the brake. The Caddy skidded out of control. He pulled frantically at the steering wheel, but the car wouldn't respond. His pulse beat in his ears. The guardrail was coming closer, closer. A scream penetrated the air as the Cadillac burst through the rail.

The last thing Jack Frost remembered was sailing through the night, behind the wheel of the old car.

At that same moment, Charlie sat at the window of the small log cabin, staring out at the rapidly falling snow. It *had* been the whitest Christmas ever, but so what? He and his mother had thrown around a few snowballs and cooked up his favorite spaghetti dinner. They tried to sing a few sappy Christmas carols but the expert sound of a certain guitar was missing. And a certain harmonica. And, of course, a certain voice. Turning those carols into the coolest, rockingest, bluesiest carols on either side of the Rockies.

Charlie watched as the snow piled up higher and higher. Maybe they really would get snowed in. But that didn't seem like much fun anymore. Not with Dad somewhere out there, when he could be here.

The snowman on the Frosts' front lawn was standing guard over only two of them now. Silent.

Staring straight ahead in his long, burgundy scarf and black porkpie hat.

As the long, sad winter began to melt into a sad, wet spring, he got smaller and smaller. The hat drooped over his head, the scarf slid to the ground.

When the last of him had soaked into the ground, the grass began to show again — bright green, tender, new. And then it got brown in the heat of summer, and soon brilliant, fiery-colored leaves were falling where the snowman had stood. And one day, a new snowflake landed right in that same spot. And another, and another . . .

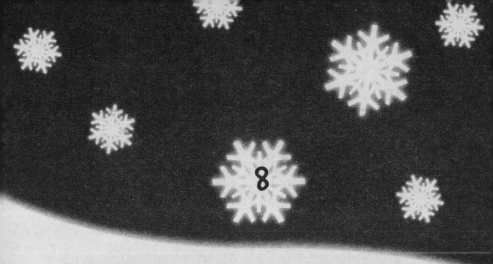

8

Vacation! Hundreds of kids were rushing the main doors of school as if the first one out won a gazillion dollars.

"Merry Christmas!" called out Ms. Joseph, the tiny, red-haired music teacher, almost getting knocked over by a student. This year, same as last.

Except it wasn't the same. Not for Charlie Frost. Charlie waited until the stampede was over. If the last one out got the consolation prize, it was his. Except he didn't think there was anything out there that could be much consolation.

He felt a blast of crisp, cold air as he stepped outside. He blinked in the bright sunshine. The light reflected off the snow almost blindingly. He didn't see the snowball until it exploded against his chest.

"Frost! Ya big dinkwad!" Rory called out from the snow-covered lawn of the school. Charlie watched him bend down and start packing another snowball. Fine. Let him. What was a little snow on your jacket?

"Forget it, Rory," he heard Pudge say from across the yard. Mitch was there, too. "He's no fun to pick on since his old man died."

"Yeah, well, it's time he got over it," Rory said meanly. "I never even met my old man."

Charlie started walking away from school. Another snowball smacked into his back. He turned around slowly.

"Rory," he said.

"What? C'mon, Frost, what?" Rory sounded excited, as if he was gearing up for a good fight.

"When you're, like, twenty-five and I'm twenty-three," Charlie asked calmly, "are you still going to be throwing snowballs at me?"

Rory didn't seem to get it. "What's that supposed to mean?" he growled.

Charlie could see Mitch and Pudge cracking up at the idea of a grown-up Rory waiting around to pound other grown-ups with snowballs. But Charlie didn't laugh along with them. When Rory turned to look at his sidekicks, they both stopped laughing instantly.

Charlie turned and headed off across the schoolyard and down the road. Alone.

Charlie skated in on the goalie from the other team as he took a shot at the puck. But his heart wasn't in it, and he barely thought about his aim. The puck went way wide. No surprise.

His teammates let out a collective groan and wasted no time chasing the action down to the other end of the rink. Charlie didn't skate after them. Instead, he cut a wide, leisurely figure eight, encircling the opposing team's goalie in one of the loops. He could feel the goalie staring at him as if he'd gone nuts. He didn't bother explaining that he just wasn't into this anymore.

"Frost?! What are you doin'?" Coach Gronic shouted at him.

Charlie shrugged. "Nothing," he said softly, as much to himself as to the coach. He didn't belong here anymore, and he knew it.

Charlie walked home from the hockey rink, his skates knotted together by the laces and dangling over one shoulder. The houses he passed were decorated for the holidays — colorful Christmas lights blinking around the windows and doors, majestic Christmas trees visible through the living room windows, an occasional menorah . . . and snowmen standing proudly, in various shapes and sizes. But Charlie wasn't anywhere close to the holiday spirit. Christmas just meant terrible, terrifying memories for him this year.

He cut into a dirt path that branched off from the road and disappeared into the woods. His mood lightened slightly as soon as he was surrounded by the huge, silent evergreens. The trees were so big, they seemed to dwarf the problems of one small person. And there was no one around to bug him about what was wrong, or ask what he was doing. Or worst of all to sneak achy-breaky, poor-Charlie-Frost glances at him when they thought he wasn't looking.

The dirt path headed into a narrow tunnel that was cut through a massive, rocky cliff. A thick fringe of long, frosted icicles graced the mouth of the tunnel. Charlie made his way around them and through the dark dampness of the tunnel. He came out at his secret spot.

It was astonishing in its beauty and tranquility — a tiny, tree-lined gem of a frozen pond, nestled in a ring of cliffs with the white-peaked foothills of the Rockies rising up in the background. A frozen waterfall gleamed its way down a ridge in one of the cliffs.

Charlie took a deep breath and swung his skates by their laces. Around they went. Around and around, gathering speed. Charlie waited until they reached the high point of their arc — and let them go.

The skates flew up into the gray sky and got tangled on a tree branch. The branch bounced several times and then stopped, bowed slightly under its new weight. The skates hung down uselessly.

Good, Charlie thought. He sat down on a fallen tree trunk and stared out at the pond. That was exactly what he wanted.

Charlie aimed the remote at the TV and flipped from channel to channel.

Next to him in the armchair, Mac — over while Gabby was out doing some last-minute Christmas shopping — was falling asleep.

There was nothing cool on TV, so Charlie

clicked the remote and the TV screen went dark. Kids' voices floated in from off the street. Happy voices. Charlie wandered over to the big picture window behind the sofa and pulled back the curtain. Natalie, Alexander, and their father were just putting the finishing touches on a snowman. Their laughter only made Charlie even sadder. He remembered the snowman he and Dad had made last year. The scarf and hat he'd lent to the big, mute guy. The way he'd looked a little like Dad. Charlie let the curtain fall closed.

What had happened to that scarf and hat, anyway? Charlie had let them sit on the snowman until he'd become a puddle on the lawn, the last, wet traces of the last happy time he and his father had spent together. Charlie glanced over at Mac, sacked out in the armchair and looking like it would take a major earthquake to wake him. He sneaked over to the front closet and poked around in the deep reaches until he found a dusty box on the floor in a back corner. He lifted the top. Yup. This was what he was looking for.

He grabbed his parka and boots and pulled them over his pajamas. Then he headed into the kitchen and rounded up a few more small items, squirreling them away in his jacket pocket. He headed out into the chilly night.

It wasn't easy rolling the three boulders of the snowman's body by himself. It took all his strength to get the middle one on top of the big one. Charlie had to get up on tiptoes to get the smaller one on top of that. But he did it. He managed. Alone. Without Dad's help.

He scouted around at the edges of the yard for two sticks that worked as arms and planted them firmly on either side of the middle ball. He arranged a wheel from one of his toy Tonka trucks, an Oreo cookie, and a Jack Frost Band button down the snowman's front. Two small pieces of charcoal were perfect as eyes. He jammed a cork in for a nose. With one swift stroke, he carved a smiling mouth with his mittened thumb.

Then the crowning touches. He ripped open the box. Inside lay Dad's porkpie hat, his burgundy scarf, and his mittens. Charlie wrapped the scarf around the snowman's neck, slipped the mittens onto the ends of the stick arms, and reached up to place the hat on top of the head.

He took a step backward to inspect his work. Okay, maybe it wasn't as even and tidy as last year's snowman. Maybe it had kind of a, well, homemade look. But it was as much a snowman as the one Natalie and her family had made across the street. Or Charlie and his father had made the year before.

Charlie stared at the snowman's face — frozen until the spring thaw in that one expression. The snowman stared back blankly. Last year, Mom had said that the snowman looked a little like Dad, with that soft black hat on its head. Charlie felt a tug of longing for his father.

He picked the box off the snow-covered lawn. Something rattled inside. Charlie peered in. It was the harmonica Dad had given him and he'd given back. He touched it with a finger and then lifted it out of the box.

Dad would be there for him whenever he played it. Yeah, sure. Charlie slipped the instrument into his pocket and headed inside.

Charlie studied the harmonica. He wanted to bring it to his lips and blow — and at the same time he didn't. He could almost hear the cascade of slippery, metallic notes — and the powerful memory of his father that went with them. But this wasn't a magical harmonica at all. No amount of blowing into it could ever, ever bring his father to his side again.

Charlie sighed and let the hand holding the harmonica drop. Then, just as quickly, he brought it up to his mouth and played a quick slide, moving his lips from one end of the instrument to the other and releasing a trickle of notes. He let his hand drop again.

Outside, the wind picked up. The leafless tree branches danced crazily, releasing a fine shower of snow into the air. Wisps of the snow began to swirl around Charlie's snowman.

Charlie watched without really focusing — vaguely aware of his snowman standing unmoving at the center of the whirl of snow. Charlie gave a start as a thick broom of lightning split the sky. *BOOM!* A cymbal crash of thunder followed.

And then the snow began to circle around the snowman with more and more force. Charlie snapped to attention as the snow spun faster and faster, creating a dizzying tornado of white around his snowman.

"I'm gonna be there. . . ." Charlie could swear

he heard the wind wailing. He gave his head a hard shake. He was imagining things.

All at once the whirlwind of snow stopped. The snowflakes blew away. Whew! Back to normal. Charlie stared at his snowman. Just the way he'd made it. And then . . . the snowman blinked.

No way! Unh-unh! Three-hundred-percent impossible! But then the snowman blinked again. And stretched his stick arms out as if he were waking up from a long nap. Charlie's eyes opened wide with astonishment and disbelief. This wasn't happening. The snowman swiveled around on his big bottom ball.

"I'm home!" it called out. Its mouth moved and its voice sounded suspiciously familiar.

Charlie stared out the window, transfixed, as the snowman waddled up toward the front door. "I'm home!" it called. "Gabby! Charlie!"

The snowman was out of Charlie's view now. The spot where he'd been standing was bare, and someone was knocking at the front door — a scratchy little stick-armed knock. "Hey! Open up!"

Charlie backed away from his window. His legs trembled. His arms shook. This was all in his head. He spun around and took a dive onto his bed, burying his head under the pillow. This wasn't real. This was his imagination.

He realized he was still clutching the harmonica. *Just blow into it and I'll be there. . . .* Couldn't be. He let the harmonica drop to the floor.

Charlie heard a *tap-tap-tap* on his window. No. He wasn't even going to look. The tapping continued.

"Charlie!" he heard a voice say.

His curiosity got the better of him. Not even daring to breathe, he got off his bed and trod over to the window. Fear hit him like a brick in the chest. The snowman! Staring in his window!

"Charlie, couldja get the door?" the snowman said. "It's me, Dad."

Charlie let out a bloodcurdling scream and snapped the blinds shut. He dove under the pillow again, pulling it tight over his ears. Just ignore it, and it will go away. Go away. Go away. . . .

As the blinds in Charlie's room fell and the window went dark, Frost got a glimpse of his reflection for the first time.

"Aaagh!" He jumped back in terror. He spun around, but there was no one behind him. No snowman, no lopsided monster sneaking up on him. He squeezed his eyes shut as he turned back around. Slowly, he opened his eyes again. He gasped. There he was. The snowman. The monster.

"No," he whispered, a horrible thought crossing his mind.

He raised his arms. The snowman raised his stick arms, too. He took off his mittens. So did the snowman. He wriggled his fingers. Ditto.

"No," he repeated, horror building inside him.

He patted his head and felt a round, slightly un-even ball. The reflection in the window did the same. He patted his belly — or the middle ball. Then down to the bottom one, toward his pants. Or where his pants would be if he'd been wearing pants. If he'd been able to wear pants. But there was nothing there. No pants, no legs to put into the pants.

"Noooooooooo!!!" Frost let out a wail of de-spair. How could it be? How could this be happen-ing? He turned this way and that, studying his reflection in Charlie's window. Three lumpy balls of snow. A huge, round, dumpy butt . . .

And then a vision in his head — crashing through the rail and sailing through the night

Jack Frost — the snowman!

Charlie waits in his bedroom
for his dad to come home.

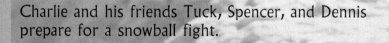

Charlie and his friends Tuck, Spencer, and Dennis
prepare for a snowball fight.

Rory Buck and his mutant snowball slingshot.

Charlie beats
Rory at his
own game.

Charlie and his dad
build a snowman.

Charlie sees a resemblance to
his father in the snowman.

Charlie asks if his dad has
brought him a present.

Jack gives Charlie a harmonica, which
he bought when Charlie was born.

Hockey players Tuck, Charlie,
and Natalie sit on the sidelines.

Charlie looks for
his dad — but
Jack isn't there.

Jack tells Charlie he has to leave for one more concert — on Christmas Eve.

One year later, with his dad gone,
Charlie builds another snowman.

Charlie finds the harmonica.

Magically, Jack comes back
to life — as a snowman
named Frost.

A snowplow is a snowman's worst
enemy: Frost tries to keep away.

Frost and Charlie race downhill on a toboggan.

Frost lifts his head [!!]
to look in the window.

Charlie skates
to a win!

Chester the dog helps Frost
get to the hockey game.

Charlie scores the winning goal — and the team celebrates!

Frost is melting!

"Thanks, Charlie. Thanks for giving me a second chance to be your dad."

air, nothing under the car's wheels . . . Crashing through the trees, snow shaking off the evergreens' branches as they were crushed by the plummeting Caddy. *CRASH!!* The car smashing into the massive trunk of a tree. The sick symphony of breaking glass and shattering metal. And then, the quiet hiss of liquid dribbling from a broken radiator hose . . .

The vision faded, but Frost could still hear the hiss of liquid. He felt something warm on his leg — well, where his leg was supposed to be. He looked down to catch Chester with his hind leg up, letting a stream of urine spray him. Frost swatted the dog's butt with one of his stick arms. "That's disgusting!"

Chester looked up at him.

"Chester, it's me," Frost said.

The little white dog let out a low growl as usual. Frost was almost glad to hear it. Some things never changed. At least Chester still knew who he was — even if Charlie was scared to death of him. Even if Frost couldn't recognize *himself* anymore.

Panicked, Charlie pushed the coffee table up against the front door. And the kitchen chairs.

"Charlie, let me in!" called that voice — his dad's voice. "I'm having kind of a bad day," it said.

The doorknob rattled. The door shook. Charlie felt his heart pounding. He glanced around the living room for something really heavy to add to the barricade in front of the door. His gaze fell on Mac, in the armchair — huge, weighty, and looking a whole lot deader right this second than that snowman trying to get into the house.

It must have been the fear surging through him — Charlie got behind the armchair and managed to shove it clear across the room. Mac let out a snore like a chainsaw, but he didn't even open an eye. Charlie wedged Mac and the chair against the pile of furniture barricading the door. He looked at Mac's oversized stomach. That ought to hold it for a while.

Then he went over to the picture window and opened the curtain the tiniest bit. Just enough to peek out. The snowman was still at the door.

"Charlie! C'mon!" he was pleading. He shook his stick arms in frustration. Chester watched him, too. Charlie could see the little terrier eyeing those waving sticks, the way he did when Charlie was getting ready to play a nice little game of fetch with him. Horrified, Charlie watched as Chester leaped up and got his mouth on one of the sticks, snatching it right out of the snowman's body and taking off.

"You've got to be kiddin' me," the snowman called after him. "Come here, boy."

Chester ran out into the middle of the street and dropped the stick. He sat there, waiting for someone to come play with him.

"When I was a human, nothing!" yelled the snowman. "Now, all of a sudden, you want to fetch."

Charlie still couldn't believe he was seeing this. He had to wake up. He gave himself a hard pinch. But the snowman and the dog were still out there. And the snowman was trying to reclaim his arm. He walked — wobbled and rolled, really — over to it and picked it up with the arm that was still attached. "Aww, you broke the bark," he yelled at the dog. "You drew sap!"

A little giggle escaped Charlie's lips. He couldn't help it. If he was dreaming, at least he'd dreamed up a talking snowman with his Dad's weird sense of humor. He'd missed that. And then he heard something else, and the giggle died on his lips. The sound of classic rock 'n' roll oldies!

Before he had time to shout out a warning, the town snowplow charged down the street, heading right for the snowman's back. Chester padded out of the way, but the snowman, busy reattaching his arm, didn't even see it coming. *BOOM!* The plow's huge shovel hit him and scooped him up.

Charlie cringed. "Ouch!"

The snowman was tossed up and down on the snow-filled shovel. The driver, unaware, headed for a wall of snow curbside to dump his load.

"Geez!" Charlie exclaimed. "That's gonna . . . sting!"

The plow smashed the snowman mercilessly into the snow. *CRUNCH! GRIND!* Charlie hid his eyes behind his hands. When he dared to look again, the plow was backing away. The snowman's body was squashed, face first, into the pile of snow. The scarf and hat stuck out uselessly from the white pile. The stick arms were motionless. The snowman was finished.

Charlie slumped to the floor. He was numb,

stunned. He couldn't have seen what he'd just seen . . . but he had. The snowman he'd built had come alive. Only to die.

Charlie let out a long, long breath. At least his dream — his nightmare — was over.

9

Frost coughed up a spray of snow. Or at least his smooshed head did. He strained his spindly arms against the wall of snow they were buried in and pushed them free. *WHOOPS!* His middle ball popped out, too, his stick arms attached to it, and bounced into the middle of the street.

Back in the wall, his poor, mashed head was still waiting to be rescued. "Don't just sit there!" it called to the ball with arms. "Gimme a hand!"

Frost pushed up on his arms — or at least the middle ball pushed up on his arms — and walked on his hands, chimpanzee-style, over to the wall of snow. He started digging. Oww! He poked his head in the eye. Yeow! Scratched himself across his soft, flattened snowball face. Ooch! Socked

66

himself right in the mouth with a mittened hand as he dug.

Finally he carved away enough of the snow wall to pull his head out. His arms picked it up and plopped it into place. "Ahhh. Feels good to be in two pieces again."

Wait a minute! Two pieces. Something was still not right about this picture. Frost looked down at himself, the middle ball sitting right on the snowy ground. His bottom half! He looked back at the wall. Snow was trickling down into the gap where Frost had dug out his two top balls. It trickled faster, became a rush of snow. And suddenly, the wall was collapsing! His bottom ball was bursting free! And geez, it was headed right, smack at him.

Frost put his stick arms up, but the bottom ball hit him as if he were a bowling pin. Down he went. And away his bottom ball rolled. Stumbling to his feet — well, not his feet, exactly — he did the chimp walk and chased his base. It rolled to a stop at the bottom of a dip in the street. Frost — the top part of him — took the opportunity to leap on top of it. His middle ball landed snugly on his bottom one. Whew! Back to normal again. If you could call this normal.

"It's bad enough my ticket was punched," he muttered to himself, as he waddled back to his spot on the lawn. "But to come back like this? I'm a musician. This is so . . . not hip."

All of a sudden, he was hit by the glare of headlights. He froze. If someone who was already frozen could be said to freeze. The Jeep. His Jeep. Gabby's Jeep. Frost felt his heart beating wildly, somewhere in there in his middle ball.

He watched Gabby pull into the driveway and get out of the car, carrying several big bags stuffed with wrapped, ribboned Christmas gifts. She began walking toward the front door. Then her gaze fell on Frost and she stopped.

"Hello, there," she said. She looked at him for a moment longer. Good for Charlie, she thought. Maybe he's snapping out of it. Her eyes went to Frost's scarf. Then to the porkpie hat perched on his head. She closed the gap between them in a few quick steps. She leaned in toward the scarf, and Frost could hear her inhale deeply.

"It's . . . nice to see these again," she whispered to herself.

Frost could smell her scent, too — the smell of her shampoo, the perfume of her skin. He could feel her nearness. Ah, bliss. Gabby, Gabby . . . he reached his scrawny stick arms toward her. . . .

She pulled back and he halted instantly. "It's good you bundled up," she said, with a far-away look on her face. "It's going to be a cold one tonight."

And then she walked away from him, and there was nothing he could do to keep her.

"Charlie, are you there?" Charlie heard his mother's voice, as she pounded on the barricaded front door.

"Mom!" He felt a rush of relief. He jumped off the sofa and raced to the door. He gave the arm-chair — with Mac still in it — a hard shove. Mac groaned as the chair moved a few inches — just enough for Charlie to dislodge the coffee table and pull away the kitchen chairs.

His mother pushed the door open — at least as far as it would go before it smacked into the arm-chair. That got Mac's eyes open. Gabby slipped into the house.

"Mom, am I glad to see you!" Charlie threw his arms around her, hugging her like a life raft in a stormy sea.

"Charlie! Have you been watching the Sci-Fi Channel again?" she asked.

"No, no!" he said, not letting go of her.

"Gabby. You're home," Mac said sleepily from the armchair. "Charlie's been great all night. . . ." His sentence trailed off as he looked around the house and took stock of where he was sitting. "What in bloody heck happened here?" he exclaimed.

Charlie gulped. "Mom, it's the snowman."

"I saw it," his mother said. "Terrific job."

"It's alive!" Charlie blurted out.

Mac stood up and shot Charlie a long look. "All right, then, I'll just be going." He grabbed the coat he'd hung up by the door and escaped through the narrow opening.

"Charlie, are you sure you're okay?" his mother asked, her voice filled with worry.

"Mom, I swear to you. He came to life and then waddled into the street and then the plow took him away." He knew it sounded crazy, but he'd seen it. With his own two eyes.

"Oh, so he must've taken a cab back here," his mother said, raising an eyebrow. She took Charlie's arm and coaxed him toward the door.

Charlie peered out. He couldn't believe it. The snowman. Standing on the lawn exactly where he'd built him. He blinked hard. When he opened his eyes, the snowman was still there. "What?!" It couldn't be. The snowman was exactly where he belonged. As if he'd never come to life in the first place. As if this whole crazy night had never happened. Charlie felt dizzy and confused. His thoughts spun wildly. Maybe it hadn't happened. Maybe it *had* been a dream. Maybe he'd been sound asleep on the sofa — just like Mac.

"Cheers, Bub," Mac called to him, as he jumped into his truck and took off.

Charlie gave a weak wave and turned to go back inside. But if he'd been asleep, then what was all this furniture doing in front of the door?

Frost wandered across the town green, deserted at this late, cold hour. The banner for this year's Shiverfest flapped overhead in the light wind. Across from the green, the clock on the church steeple tolled out eleven gongs. "It's eleven o'clock. Do you know where your snowman is?" Frost intoned like a television announcer.

Over by the huge Christmas tree, all lit up in the

middle of the green, someone had built a family of silent, still snowpeople. A mommy snowperson, a daddy snowperson, and two little snowkids. Frost waddled and rolled on over to them. Once he'd rock 'n' rolled. Now he waddled and rolled. "Why me?" Frost said to them. "Why a snowman? Is it just because of the name Jack Frost? Because that's not even clever. . . ."

He gave the daddy snowman a poke, and his head plopped off. He watched it sink into the snow. "I guess I'm alone in the walking, talking department," he said. He turned his back on his fellow snowpeople and kept waddling. He reached the sidewalk. He could see that, behind him, snaking across the green, he'd left a thick trail in the snow.

"This hurts," he muttered to himself as he kept moving down the street. He didn't know where he was going, but he was going. No use standing around on his lawn all night longing for Charlie and Gabby. He felt a warm tear running down his face, freezing quickly into a tiny icicle.

Suddenly, he was bathed in a blinding light. A roaring sound filled his ears. The light got bigger, brighter, swallowing him up. A heavenly light coming to take him where he belonged? Or send him the other way? "What am I?" he called out, frightened. "Someone help me! Just give me a sign!" He stared directly into the blazing light. "That's right! I'm a frozen freak of nature!" he cried.

The lights swept past him, and as his eyes adjusted, he saw he'd been staring into the headlights of an old black Toyota Land Cruiser. His fear dissolved. Right — some heavenly sign. The van drove by him slowly. He peered into the driver's side and saw a familiar face.

"Sid?! Sid Gronic? Is that you?" It certainly looked like Sid, except instead of Sid's beefy scowl, his face was frozen in absolute shock as he stared at the talking snowman.

Frost started waddling toward the van. "Oh, man, Sid," he called out. "I've been hearing great things about you."

"Aaaagh!" Sid let out a cry of bloody murder and threw the van into reverse, screeching backward down the street.

"Thanks for the help, Sid," the snowman said to himself.

10

In the crisp, early morning sunshine, Charlie walked slowly around the snowman. He'd waited impatiently until Mom had left for work. Now the coast was clear. He thrust his hand into the snowman's face. "Boo!" he screamed. The snowman stared vacantly from his coal eyes.

Charlie turned and ran toward the house. "You're gonna have to do better than 'boo,'" he thought he heard the snowman snicker.

He whirled around. The snowman was frozen in one place. This guy thought he was so clever, so slick. Well, Charlie could be clever, too.

He emerged from the house a few minutes later, brandishing his mother's hair dryer like a gun. The long orange extension cord snaked back into the house. He took aim at the snowman. "Who are you? What do you want?"

The snowman played at his frozen game. Charlie switched the hair dryer on. "I know you're alive, so you better start talking." He held the dryer straight out, as the warm air streaming from its nozzle quickly dented the snowman's belly.

Suddenly the snowman screamed. "No, not the Sunbeam!" He moved his mittened hands over the melting spot and retreated.

Charlie screamed. It was happening again. The snowman was alive! The snowman was talking!

"Charlie, it's me — Dad!" the snowman said. "I can explain everything. Well, not the part about me being a snowman . . ."

The hair dryer slipped from Charlie's hands. He didn't stop screaming as he bolted out of his yard, down the street, and into the woods. He ran as hard and fast as he could pump his legs. He put as much distance as he could between himself and the snowman who thought he was his dad.

Charlie didn't stop running until he was deep in the woods. And he only stopped then because he heard voices.

"Go pick on someone as dumb as you!" Natalie! He recognized her voice right away. He took a few more steps and saw Rory and his two stooges playing "keep away" with her purple ski hat. Natalie jumped up to grab it out of Rory's hand, but she missed.

"I hope you know that school bullies make up seventy-five percent of our prison population," she scolded. Then she spied Charlie and grinned. Help had arrived.

Or so Natalie thought. Charlie just stood there. It had been a long time since he'd had enough get-up-and-go to fight the forces of evil. The grin slipped off Natalie's face.

Mitch spotted Charlie, too. "Look, it's our little hero," he said snidely.

"Don't worry about him anymore," Rory snickered. "He's not even in the game." He dangled the hat just close enough to Natalie to make her lunge for it. But he pulled it away before she could get her fingers on it. Charlie stood there watching as Rory filled Natalie's hat with snow. "Okay, Natalie. Here's your hat," he said, laughing nastily.

All of a sudden, a snowball winged past Charlie

from behind and smacked Rory in the nose. Rory looked at Charlie, astonished. "Frost! So you *do* want a piece of me." He signaled to Mitch and Pudge to start packing ammunition. "Thought you learned your lesson, Frost. Guess it's time for a refresher course."

Rory and his boys raised their snowballs. Charlie braced himself. And then — *BOOM!* Another snowball hit Rory. Who had thrown that?

Charlie whirled around. The snowman! Right in back of him! Positioned behind a tree so only Charlie could see him. He gave Charlie a wink as he packed a big, double snowball and hurled it. It split right in midair into two separate balls, nailing Pudge and Mitch at the same second.

Rory threw a snowball at Charlie. Charlie ducked. The snowball whizzed past him but hit the snowman in the head, knocking his porkpie hat off. Charlie saw his dent of a mouth pucker in anger.

"Okay! Shovel this!" Frost hissed under his breath. Now he was mad. He pulled on the end of his scarf as if he were pulling the starter cord on a lawn mower. His stick arms started going around and around like windmills, scooping up snowballs with each turn and flinging them at the bullies. Faster, faster, faster . . . a storm of fire. "Don't mess with the wizard of blizzard!" Charlie heard him say.

Rory and company were pelted with snowballs, one after another. They screamed, dodging, and bumping into each other, and running this way and that. Charlie took the opportunity to make his exit. He wasn't sure who he was running from — the bullies or the snowman.

"He's getting away!" Rory yelled, pointing at Charlie and going after him.

Charlie raced up a steep hill. Looking over his shoulder, he could see that the snowman's attack was running out of steam — or snow, rather. Natalie had escaped, but the bullies were after Charlie, now.

"Get him!" Rory called.

Charlie kept climbing as fast as he could. Rory, Pudge, and Mitch were close on his tail, whooping like the animals they were. Charlie scrambled to the top of the hill — and gasped. He was trapped! The hill dropped off sharply, plummeted straight down for at least three stories and then gave way to a steep downhill slope.

"Don't worry!" he heard his father's voice —

well, the snowman's voice — calling out to him from somewhere nearby. But one of Rory's icy snowballs smacked into him, hard. He felt himself losing his balance. He waved his arms and tried to recover, but his feet slid out from under him. He started going down . . . down . . . headed right over the ridge and into the void.

Charlie let out a bloodcurdling scream. He managed to grab onto a branch jutting out over the ridge. He clung to it, terrified, his body hanging down in thin air.

"I've got you covered, bud!" Charlie looked down. The snowman was at the very base of the ridge, waving at him from a flotilla of snow saucers, toboggans, and sleds that had been abandoned there. Charlie looked back the way he'd come. The bullies were closing in on him.

Down below, the snowman heaved a big toboggan sideways onto a sled to form a seesaw. He jumped onto one end. Then, in a quick-fingered maneuver, the snowman managed to unscrew his top two balls and hurl the bottom one onto the other end of the seesaw. The rest of him went boomeranging up into the air toward Charlie. "And, it's a high fly ball!" he sang out.

Rory and the thugs were now close enough to let loose with a volley of snowballs. They struck Charlie one after another. His fingers were slipping. He was losing his grip on the branch. He tried to hold on, but his hands gave way. He screamed. He was falling, falling. . . .

Just then the high flying top part of the snowman soared up and grabbed him with those two stick arms. They went plummeting down together — down, down . . . whoosh! Charlie felt something mushy give way underneath him. He looked down. They had made a cushioned landing on the snowman's bottom ball.

Safe! The snowman patted at his bottom, pushing it back into shape. "Sometimes it's good to have a big butt," he said.

Charlie couldn't believe this. Saved by a talking snowman. But before he had a chance to think about it, he saw Rory and his gang preparing to launch a mammoth ice boulder from up on the ridge.

"Quick!" said the snowman. They jumped onto the toboggan and took off down the slope. Charlie heard the wind in his ears. They sailed. But so did the boulder, gathering size and speed as it ripped down the snow-covered slope.

Charlie laughed in triumph. But it was too soon. Hot on their trail were Rory on his snowboard, Mitch on a saucer, and Pudge on a snow scooter.

"Whatever happened to plain old sledding?" the snowman asked.

"Do something," Charlie implored. "Zap 'em into ice!"

"Get real!" answered the snowman. "I don't even have *pockets*!" They sped downhill. Rory and his boys followed close behind.

They took a sharp, narrow curve, the toboggan banking like a luge on an Olympic track. And suddenly they found themselves zooming right at the enormous, gaping mouth of a storm-drain tunnel.

There was no room on either side of the drain to escape. They had no choice but to rocket straight into the tunnel. Charlie and the snowman screamed together! The toboggan picked up even more speed on the frozen, icy metal.

In back of them, there was a matched set of top-volume screams. Charlie heard Mitch and Pudge collide outside the drainpipe opening, in a big way. Well, two down.

But the trip wasn't over yet. The toboggan kept going, shooting off the bottom of the pipe and into the daylight again, sailing through midair, briefly, then gliding onto the snow.

Charlie felt the wind knocked out of him as they came down hard. Way too hard. The toboggan started shaking. Charlie could see a split in the wood. It was coming apart!

At just that second, he heard a war whoop. Behind them, Rory was flying off the top of the drainpipe, doing a 360 on his snowboard, and coming down not far from them. They raced forward. "Look out!" Charlie screamed. Straight ahead, blocking the entire path, was a tightly clustered group of giant evergreens. Too tight for a wide toboggan to make it through.

But the snowman seemed to take it in stride. "Time to split!" he announced cheerfully. He slammed his foot down on the ground — or some part of his bottom ball where his foot would have been. The split in the wood widened. The toboggan cracked right down the middle, breaking into two narrower, ski-shaped pieces of wood.

Snowboards! The snowman got up on one of them. Charlie followed his lead and straddled the other. They zigzagged through the maze of trees.

But Rory was gaining on Charlie. And he was an expert snowboarder. "Hey, bud!" the snowman called out to Rory.

Rory looked over and really saw the snowman for the first time. Yes, a snowman. Riding a make-shift snowboard and talking to him. His eyes widened. His jaw went slack. The snowman waved at him. Rory let out a whimper and lost his balance. He boarded right toward a thick branch sticking out of the ground. The branch caught him neatly between the legs. Rory let out a howl as he was stopped cold, the branch pressing against his body from his crotch to his nose. And then . . . *SNAP!* The branch gave way, and Rory fell face first into a deep snowbank.

Charlie let out a cry of glee. He and the snowman wove gracefully down the rest of the hill on their toboggan-snowboards. Powdery plumes of snow flew up in their wakes. The sun shone through the trees in dappled patches, as they left their pursuers far behind them.

At the bottom of the hill, Charlie did a graceful

hockey stop on his board. The snowman did, too. "That was too cool!" Charlie exclaimed. His smile stretched right off his face. "Awesome!"

"You ain't kidding!" the snowman agreed. "Man, there's an advantage to being built this way. It really helped me set edge. That was fun!" The snowman acted out an exaggerated turn on his board.

Charlie watched him. The rush was beginning to wear off. And here he was . . . with this guy. "You almost got me killed back there," he said quietly.

"Yeah, well, I saved your butt, too," the snowman said.

"So, I'm supposed to believe you're my dad?"

"Hey, I'm having a little trouble believing it myself, okay?"

Charlie felt a shudder of sadness. "Well, he died a year ago."

"I know. I was there."

"You're nuts," Charlie told the snowman.

"Great," the snowman muttered to himself. "He doesn't believe me. As if I don't have enough on my plate already with the stick arms and the humongous butt . . ."

"And the dippy walk," Charlie reminded him.

"Is it really that bad?"

"Well . . . not for a snowman," Charlie conceded. He eyed the snowman. "If you're really my dad, then how did my hamster die?"

"Heart attack."

"Vacuum cleaner," Charlie corrected him.

"I bet it had a heart attack on the way in," the snowman cracked.

"How'd I break my retainer?" Charlie pressed.

"You put it in your back pocket and then sat on it at school."

"Trick question," Charlie said, feeling his anger spark. "I never had a retainer. What position do I play in hockey?"

"That's easy. Winger. Right wing . . . I mean, you used to play center but —"

"Wrong!" Charlie spat out.

"What?" The snowman was shocked.

"They moved me to defense a while ago," Charlie said.

"Aww, really? You were a great wing-man, Charlie-boy, you shouldn't be on defense."

Charlie tensed. "What did you call me?"

"Charlie-boy," the snowman said. And there was no doubt about it — it was his father's voice.

Charlie looked into the snowman's coal eyes. Somehow those smudgy pieces of coal managed to be moist and shiny and filled with unshed tears. Charlie could see his reflection in them. "Dad!"

And then they were wrapping each other in a wet, huge, mushy hug. A hug that had been a whole, sad, angry, terrible year in coming. Charlie's eyes were filled with tears, too.

A chunk of snow came off in his hand. He took a step away. "This is . . . too weird!"

"Hey, buddy, you were the one who played on the magic harmonica," said the snowman . . . his dad.

"I thought you made that up," Charlie said.

"So did I." The snowman — Dad — shook his big, round head. "Let's talk, Charlie-boy. Someplace private . . . and cold."

The snowman basked in front of the open freezer in Charlie's kitchen — in their kitchen. Chester growled at him. It was good to have Dad home.

"Charlie, how's your mom doing?" Dad asked.

"She's okay," Charlie said. It wasn't as if either of them had been having much fun this year.

"You helping her out around here?"

"Uh-huh. I shovel the driveway and take out the garbage."

"Good."

"She moved a picture of you right next to her bed." Or, rather, a picture of the way he used to look. But Charlie didn't add this, thinking it was kind of rude.

"Really?" His father sounded very pleased.

"Last week she baked these double chocolate chip cookies and even played hockey with me in the driveway. She's pretty decent."

Dad smiled his snowman smile. "Yeah, she is pretty decent," he said. "I can tell you, snowman or human, there's nobody like your mom."

"You want me to give her a hug for you?"

"Yeah, please." Frost was quiet for a moment.

Suddenly, they heard the sound of a car pulling into the driveway. "Mom's home!" Charlie said.

"No! She cannot see me like this! Well, nobody can see me like this, but especially her."

"Why?" asked Charlie. Okay, Dad as a snowman had been a little hard to take at first, but he'd gotten over it. Sort of.

But Frost shook his snowball head. "She's been through enough. You've got to help me, Charlie. I promise, I'll make it up to you."

A promise. One of Dad's promises. Charlie felt a cold shot of anger. "You used to make a lot of those, remember?"

Dad frowned. Just as Charlie heard Mom's key in the door. "Charlie?" she called out. "Wow, it's freezing in here."

Charlie and his snowman father looked at each other in panic. "Just a minute!" Charlie yelled to his mother. Now what?! He started throwing the food back in the freezer.

"Charlie, why are all the windows open?" she called.

"Do something!" his father said.

Charlie raced into the living room. His mother was closing the windows and turning up the thermostat. "Charlie, what's going on?!"

"Science fair project," Charlie ad-libbed.

"You're kidding."

"No, uhh . . . it's all about what it's like to live in an igloo," Charlie managed.

His mother shook her head and walked toward the kitchen.

"No!" Charlie said.

"No?" Gabby Frost wrinkled her brow and went into the kitchen, anyway. "Why is this floor wet?"

Charlie followed after her. The snowman — Dad — was gone, but there was a puddle in the middle of the linoleum tile floor. He grabbed a dish towel and wiped the water furiously. "Mom, Eskimos have wet floors, duh!" He tried his best to sound convincing.

His mother opened the door to the broom closet. The mop seemed to jump out at her. She caught it and gave a little jump back. Charlie knew his father was in there. "Um, Mom, there's something I have to tell you," he said, drawing her attention.

"What?" His mother turned, looking at him as he crouched down on the floor with the dish towel. While she was turned toward Charlie, the snowman sneaked out of the kitchen and slid into the living room toward the door.

"Uh, well . . . uhm . . ."

"Earth to Charlie," his mother said.

"Oh. This whole science fair thing was Natalie's idea." Charlie said the first thing that popped into his head. "Talk to her."

"Well, just tell Natalie the next experiment is at her house." Mom paused and looked out the kitchen window. Charlie looked out, too. The snowman was back on the lawn, in his place.

Mom shook her head hard. "I could have sworn he wasn't there when I came in. I think I need a day off," she said.

*　　*　　*

Charlie sat on the sofa and clicked at the TV remote. A weird-looking black-and-white movie. He clicked. A rerun of *Wheel of Fortune*. Click. Flames and mayhem on the screen. Some kind of disaster movie. He paused and turned around, looking out the open curtain to check with his snowman father.

Frost looked in at the screen and cringed, making an overblown "hot" motion by wiping at his forehead with his mittened hand. Okay, no flames for Dad. Charlie clicked. *Frosty the Snowman*?! He and his father both shook their heads hard. Click.

A newsman appeared on the screen, reporting live from Medford Town Hall. "And you say this snowman spoke to you?"

Coach Gronic appeared on the television. "Yes. And he knew my name!"

Charlie shot his father a glance. The snowman laughed.

Back on TV, Sid Gronic disappeared, and the local news studio came into focus. The camera zoomed in on Medford's petite blond weatherperson. "Folks in the Rocky Mountain states may not be in for such a white Christmas, after all. A strong warm front is moving in."

Charlie was distracted by his mother as she entered the room with a red Christmas candle and placed it on the sill of the picture window. "Was that Sid Gronic I heard. . . ." her voice trailed off. Charlie saw her staring at Frost. "Why is the snowman facing this way?" she asked.

Oops. "I wanted to . . . even out his tan," Charlie fudged.

His mother shook her head and closed the curtain. "Oh . . . was that Sid Gronic I heard on TV?"

"Yeah."

"What was he talking about?"

Charlie shrugged. "Oh . . . nothing," he said, trying not to laugh.

Mom took a seat next to him on the sofa. "Well, I was talking to Sid yesterday at the bank, and he said you quit the team."

The laughter died on Charlie's lips.

"Charlie, you didn't tell me," his mother went on. "Do you want to talk?"

"About what?"

"I don't know. This hockey thing. Or maybe how you're doing in school . . . You tell me."

"Mom, I'm trying to watch the weather."

"I just want to know how you're feeling. Sometimes talking about things can help you feel better."

"Mom, I feel fine," Charlie insisted.

His mother stroked his hair. "What am I going to do with you, little bear?" she asked.

Frost had heard it all. And seen it all. Seen Gabby's look of worry. Heard the tender way she'd tried to talk to their son. Even though she'd closed the curtains, he'd found a way to look in on his family. "It'll be all right, Gabby. I'm here now," he said quietly.

He glanced down. His scrawny arms held his head as high as they could, so he could peer in at Charlie and Gabby through the little spaces between the curtain rings. His detached head looked down at the rest of his snowball self. "I'm here now. . . ." he repeated. "Sort of."

12

Morning sunshine spilled into Charlie's room and onto his blue rug. Charlie peered out his window. Frost stood motionless in his spot on the front lawn. Good. Charlie pulled on his boots and grabbed his parka. He tiptoed into the kitchen and beat a hasty retreat out the back door.

And smacked right into the bloated snowman who'd waddled around the house to catch him in the act. Charlie let out a yelp.

"I invented the backdoor escape, okay?" Frost reminded Charlie. "Where are you going?"

"Somewhere *alone*. To think," Charlie said.

"About what?"

"Well, since you showed up, Rory Buck wants to

kill me, Mom thinks I'm nuts, and I'm pretty sure that my dad's a snowman."

"Yeah, yesterday was kind of a rough day," Frost said.

Gee, thank you very much for that piece of wisdom, Charlie thought crankily. He pushed past the snowman and headed down the driveway. The snowman toddled after him.

"Quit following me. You can't just waltz through town in broad daylight," Charlie said.

"I don't waltz. I waddle." The snowman overplayed his teetering bowling pin of a walk.

Charlie resisted laughing. "Good. Everyone'll see you. They'll take you away and cut you up into little numbered ice cube trays."

"If that's the danger of going with you, then I'll take my chances," Frost said, seriously for once.

Charlie let out a long, steamy breath in the crisp morning air. It wasn't going to be so easy to shake this guy. And maybe, deep down, he didn't really want to.

Charlie tugged the snowman down the wooded path on his sled. Into the tunnel fringed with icicles. And out onto his private winter wonderland.

"I can't believe I let you talk me into this," he told the snowman.

"I think we look kind of cute," Frost cracked.

The worst had been pulling Frost through town, past the library, the church, the town hall. Past the bank where Mom worked. Charlie sure hoped his mother hadn't glanced out her window as he'd gone by. And his face got hot just thinking about pulling the snowman past the town green, where Tuck and Dennis were playing hockey on the duck pond. Charlie could only imagine what they were thinking. *Ditched by Charlie Frost for a dumpy snowman.*

But now the peaceful magic of this place worked its spell — the shimmering frozen pond and waterfall, the cliffs and mountains and trees surrounding them. Charlie started to relax.

"Charlie, this is cool," Frost said.

"Yeah, I've been here a lot this year." Charlie sat down on the log. Frost wobbled over and sat down, too. He gave a long sigh.

"You know, Charlie, the night I crashed . . . I wasn't on the way to the job. . . . I turned around. I was on the way to come see you."

"Mom told me that."

"It's true," Frost said.

"So, why were you coming back?" Charlie asked.

"Well, I decided that playing music was important, but that you and Mom were more important."

Charlie listened to the familiar rise and fall of his father's voice. It really was comforting to hear it again. "Sorry I gave you back your harmonica," he said after a while.

"Oh, no. Don't be." The snowman — Dad — put one of his stick arms around Charlie's shoulder. "You did a good thing. You were honest."

Overhead, there was a metallic tinkling, like a set of wind chimes. Charlie looked up. His skates! Still hanging in the tree. His father looked up, too.

"You know, Charlie, it's a good thing to have a dream, too. A really good thing." He looked at his son with his coal eyes. "Why'd you quit hockey?"

Charlie shrugged. "Hockey's not that great."

"Right. That's why the last person you see before you go to sleep every night is Wayne Gretzky on your wall," Frost pointed out. "C'mon, let me teach you the J-shot."

Yeah, that's what Dad had said right before he'd

gone off and died. "I don't think so," Charlie mumbled.

"Oh. I see. It's like that. Okay," Frost said, punctuating his words with exaggerated, sad, mopey-eyed faces. He jumped up and started singing a rocking, bluesy tune. "Time to get off your big, fat butt, time to fasten those skates . . ." He spun around and strummed an air guitar. "Dad's a snowman and it's got you down? Well, this snowman really rates."

Charlie felt himself smiling. He couldn't help it. The snowman had all his father's moves down. The particular way he had of dancing while he played, the little shuffle into a spin. He even blew into an invisible harmonica and made a slippery *wah-wah* sound that managed to imitate a harmonica pretty well. The cool, rocking star of the Jack Frost Band as a snowman!

"Okay, okay, enough!" Charlie laughed. "Stop! I'll do it just to get you to stop singing."

A few minutes later, they were out on the pond, each with a tree branch in place of a hockey stick. Dad had used the seesaw boomerang move from the toboggan chase to heave his top two balls into the air and pick Charlie's skates out of the tree. Several flat stones made good pucks.

"Boy, this was easier when I had legs," Frost said, positioning his hockey stick branch by the puck. "Okay, the trick to the J-shot is to stay relaxed — keep your arms and wrists straight but loose." He demonstrated. Charlie followed him with his own branch and puck.

"But instead of just swinging at the puck, pull it back toward you, and then whip it right back out, like the letter J," his father explained. He swung, snapping his twig wrists, and . . . his arms went flying off, the mittens still gripping the hockey stick.

"Ouch, that's gotta sting," Charlie said, suppressing a giggle.

"Just go get my arms, wise guy," Frost said.

Charlie retrieved his arms, laughing.

"You're laughin', huh?" his dad said as Charlie reattached the arms. "You know something? That's good! Stay relaxed like that."

"But I got to remember . . ." Charlie said. "Straight arms and wrists and —"

"Don't remember," his father instructed. "Just let her rip. Don't think, buddy."

Charlie skated away uncertainly. Don't think about the shot?

"C'mon. You realize you're playing hockey with a snowman, right?"

Charlie laughed. He had the puck on his stick in front of him. Still chuckling, he pulled it back toward him and then snapped his wrists. He drilled the puck straight and hard. It sailed across the ice. He felt a beat of proud surprise.

Frost caught the puck. He was grinning. "Attababy, Charlie! Beea-utiful!"

"I did it!" Charlie exclaimed.

"Yes, you did." Frost sounded just as proud.

"But wait, you blocked it," Charlie realized, with a breath of disappointment. Frost had caught the puck like a goalie at the net.

"Yeah, life's full of setbacks," his dad said. "Look at me — I'm a snowdrift with arms. You can give up or, hey, you can keep firin' the puck, bud."

Well, he *had* gotten the shot off just the way he'd wanted to, Charlie thought. And was he going to let a lopsided snowman stop him? Even if it was his dad? "Gimme that puck," he said.

Frost smiled and dropped the puck.

*   *   *

Okay. He had it down. Charlie got his stick on the puck and glanced over at his father. Frost was defending a net they'd put together with pine tree branches.

"I-I-It's snowtime!" his dad sang out, like an emcee at the start of a stage show.

Arms and wrists relaxed but straight. Pull back. Out again. Wham! Charlie let 'er fly. The snowman lunged at the puck, but it whizzed by him and hit the pine branch net. A perfect J-shot! "This Frost ain't lost!" rapped the snowman.

Charlie grinned, skating right. He took the puck from a different angle. *BOOM!* "That was pucktastic!" his father announced.

Left. *BANG!* "I'm gettin' a headache!" Frost said as Charlie moved another perfect shot right past him.

He shot again. Yes! "Big stick!" his father yelled.

Again. "Gnarly Charlie! Are you sure you're only twelve?"

Charlie was hot. He was on fire. He couldn't miss. He skated around the pond and gathered up three flat stone pucks, lining them up at different angles to the net. He took a deep breath. Then, *BISH, BASH, BOOM!* He skated from one to the next without pausing for a second, sending each puck flying.

One, two, three! The pucks shot right at Frost at top speed. He didn't even have time to roll out of the way. They blasted straight through his middle ball in quick succession, leaving three round holes in his bottom two balls. Frost was knocked flat on his big, snowy butt. He still managed to yell out his approval. "There you go! Whewww!"

Charlie skated over immediately. "Are you all right?" He grabbed a handful of snow and began plugging up his dad's holes.

"I'm good, buddy." Frost patted the new snow into place. "I think you got the J-shot down."

He and Charlie looked at each other and laughed.

13

Charlie pulled Frost up his driveway on the sled. Mac's pickup was parked at the curb.

"Be careful. Mom and Mac are here," Charlie warned him, as the snowman hopped off at his usual spot on the snow-covered lawn.

"That was a blast, huh?" Frost said.

"Yeah. Thanks for showing me the J-shot."

"I can't wait to see you use it," his father said. "And I don't mean in the driveway, either. I mean a real game. You've got to get back on the team."

Charlie shook his head. "I don't know about that."

"I do. I think you're letting down yourself and your friends," his dad lectured.

Hold on. He was being lectured by a snowman?!
"But wait a second . . ." Charlie said.

"No buts, okay? Now, about your schoolwork."

Charlie was more amazed than angry. Learning the J-shot from an overgrown snowcone was one thing. Getting scolded by him was another. "What about it?"

"Hey, I saw your report card. You've got some serious jammin' to do, buddy," Frost said.

Okay, so Charlie's grades had fallen. It had been a tough year. And this guy, of all people, wasn't in any position to be wagging his finger. Or his mitten. "What is this, a lecture?" Charlie asked, upset. "*Now* you give me a lecture?"

Frost didn't back off. "And another thing. I'm a little worried about your mom," he said. "How many Christmas lights has she hung?"

Charlie glanced at the house. Mom and Mac were peeking out from behind the curtain. Whatever. The red Christmas candle was on the inside windowsill, unlit, and one measly string of lights blinked pitifully over the door.

Charlie turned back to Snowdad. "Why are you pointing that out?" he asked, tightly.

"Because you've got responsibilities now, Charlie. You've got to have the guts to face them. You're the one who's got to watch out for Mom. You've got to straighten things out with your friends, too."

Charlie's anger mounted. Dad, talking about family responsibility? "Hey! I'm only twelve years old! I . . . I can't handle this!"

Charlie left his sled on the lawn and ran into the house.

But things weren't any better in there. His mom was deep into a serious talk with Mac — about Charlie. The minute they realized he was in the house, they looked up guiltily.

"Hey, Charlie," Mac managed.

Charlie nodded a little hello. His mother poked Mac, as if reminding him he had something else to say.

"I was just heading over to the Shiverfest," Mac said. "I thought maybe you'd like to come with me."

Charlie frowned. For what? One of those "man-to-man" talks? He'd had quite enough of that from his frozen friend, thank you very much.

His mother shot him a long look. "Or . . . you can just stay here."

Charlie thought about the snowman out on

the lawn. He wasn't sure he wanted to hang here, either.

The Shiverfest was as lame as Charlie knew it would be. The Santa's Village looked just like shop class at school — with a bunch of adults in elf costumes. Santa, some wiry dude in a red suit that was way too big for him, was the worst.

Charlie felt a stab of jealousy when he and Mac passed the Woodcutting Contest. All his friends had entered — with their dads. Everyone but him, and he noticed, standing off to the side, Rory Buck.

Mac groaned when he and Charlie ambled over to a makeshift stage. There, a sappy band was massacring "The Little Drummer Boy."

Suddenly, Charlie turned to Mac. No way did he want a "man-to-man" talk — but he *did* need to know one thing. "You think my dad wanted me to be a musician?"

"I think," Mac answered Charlie, "more than anything, he wanted you to be what *you* wanted to be. He didn't care what that was. Whatever made you happy." Mac gently tapped Charlie's heart with his finger.

"Really?" Charlie said with a little smile.
"Really."

*   *   *

Charlie lay in bed, Mac's words echoing through his head. *More than anything, your Dad wanted you to be whatever made you happy. . . .*

What an unbelievable day. Charlie let out a long, deep sigh. Snowdad. Maybe Charlie had been too hard on him for sounding off with that lecture. His father the snowman was only trying to help.

And the thing was, it had been fun playing hockey on the frozen pond. Charlie missed it. And the school stuff — it honestly hadn't felt good to bring home a rotten report card this year.

Maybe it was time for Charlie to get on with things, too.

Dad might be an overgrown triple-scoop snow-cone, but Charlie still had a few things to learn from the guy.

14

Charlie burst out of the house with his hockey equipment. It was a beautiful day. The sun was bright and warm on his face. He looked at the snow-man on his lawn. He seemed a little drippy around the temples and forehead, as if he were sweating.

But Frost grinned at Charlie and called a cheery, "Good morning!"

Charlie went over to him, dragging his hockey stuff. "I did a lot of thinking about what you said, Dad. You're right."

Across the street, Sid Gronic's Land Cruiser pulled up in front of Natalie's house and honked. Charlie could see Tuck and his other hockey buddies inside. He turned back to his father. "When you taught me the J-shot, it wasn't just about hockey, was it?"

"What do you think?" his dad asked.

"I think I've got something to do," Charlie said. He turned and headed for Coach Gronic's van.

"Charlie? When do they drop the puck?" he heard his father call out behind him.

Charlie looked back over his shoulder. "Eleven-thirty. Dad, you don't have to be there."

"I'll be there."

"Really?" Charlie had heard this before. Of course, his father was — well, different now.

"Remember, arms and wrists . . ."

". . . straight but relaxed," Charlie finished, with a grin. Maybe Dad really would make it this time. He sprinted across the street and tapped on one of the Land Cruiser's windows. "Hey, guys. Hey, Coach."

Coach Gronic rolled down his window. "Charlie."

"I'd like to come back on the team."

"What?!" said Spencer, from inside the car.

"You ditched us, Charlie, remember?" Tuck added.

Dennis looked at Charlie. "I don't know, Charlie," he said.

"I do," said a new voice. Natalie! She was lugging her hockey equipment up to the van. "I say we let him back on the team. Everybody deserves a second chance."

The boys in the van looked at one another. One by one, they nodded. Coach Gronic gave a short nod, too.

Charlie smiled. He glanced at his father. He distinctly saw Dad wink a coal eye. As Charlie climbed in, he saw Coach Gronic staring at the snowman, a look of fearful disbelief on his face. As Coach Gronic peeled away from the curb, Charlie thought he heard him let out a little whimper.

What Frost wouldn't have given for a little vacation in the Arctic right about now. He struggled across the lawn, his lumpy body sagging and melting in the unseasonably warm weather. Talk about crash diets! He was losing weight by the minute. "It's no use," he mumbled to himself. "I'm liquidated." He could barely get himself down the driveway, let alone to the hockey stadium.

Chester trotted over to him. He raised his leg.

Oh, no! Like Frost really needed this, on top of everything else. But then the terrier reconsidered and padded over to one of the trees near Mrs. Wilkins's lawn. Suddenly, Frost got an idea.

He waited until Chester had finished and then dragged himself over, oozing snow all the way. He took the little dog by the collar. "Listen, Chet. You've got to help me. I've got a promise to keep."

Chester barked—not the usual low growl. Good sign. Frost smiled and scratched the dog's head.

Charlie had the puck. He was going, going. . . .

"Just like old times, Frost." Charlie heard Rory's voice come from behind. Suddenly, Rory was body-slamming him. Charlie stumbled and went down onto the hard ice.

Rory guffawed as he skated off with the puck. Charlie pushed to his feet, ready to chase Rory down. But the big bully was already getting off a shot as hard and fast as a bullet.

In front of the goal Tuck ducked in fear. The puck slammed into the net. The dried-apple score-keeper just shook her head and rang up the goal. Devils: 1, Mountaineers: 0.

But Charlie wasn't going to let Rory stop him this time. He was a new man since the J-shot. He glanced up into the bleachers and around the stadium. No snowmen in porkpie hats. But, hey, he told himself, it was still early in the game. And Dad was never, ever on time.

As the action started again, Charlie charged the puck. Got his hockey stick on it. He heard his father's voice in his head. *Don't think, buddy. Just let 'er rip.* He did. *PING!* It bounced off the post. Not quite. But not bad, either, Charlie thought.

It was a new day for Charlie Frost. He just hoped his dad made it in time to see his next shot.

"On, Dancer on Prancer on Donder and Blitzen . . ." Frost called out from his seat on Charlie's sled. Chester was tethered to the front of it by a rope, pulling it along like one of Santa's reindeer. Water ran down Frost's cheeks, and his body was as shaky as a bowl of vanilla pudding in the strong morning sun. But at least he was getting somewhere.

Chester tugged the sled down a gentle hill and across a field. "So far, so good. Hey, Chester?"

Whew! But what a nasty, mild day. Frost unwound his scarf and wrung it out. Whoa! A torrent of water came out, like a river in the spring thaw. "Okay, maybe I was a little hasty," Frost mumbled.

Chester drew the sled to a hill, and he stopped. Frost snapped the rope. Chester didn't move.

I *am* going to see my boy play, Frost thought. He spotted a thin sapling branch on the ground near them. He stretched his stick arm to pick it up and snapped the branch in the air like a whip. CRACK!

Chester let out a yelp and took off. The sled jerked forward. "Heeyaaa!" yelled Frost.

Rory stuck out his skate in front of Dennis. Dennis tripped and went flying, splat onto the ice. Rory grabbed the puck and got ready to drive it toward a cowering Tuck, at the Mountaineers' net.

No way, Charlie thought, sneaking up on Rory from behind. Rory brought his hockey stick back to shoot. In skated Charlie and stole the puck away. Yes!

Charlie grinned as the old scorekeeper looked absolutely stunned. Holding at 1–0. The Mountaineers still had a chance. Hey, this was fun! Charlie scanned the bleachers again. The crowd was cheering for him.

But he didn't see his snowdad anywhere in that crowd. Charlie's new enthusiasm melted just a little bit.

The gleaming, glass-and-metal hockey stadium was right in front of Frost's eyes. The Emerald City — closer than ever! There was only one problem. And what a problem. To get to it, you had to cross a huge, steamy parking lot.

Chester and Frost stood at the edge of it, looking across. The black asphalt was just soaking up the sun like a sponge. The sled was useless. And the lot was immense. Frost let out a wet moan. As far as he was concerned, it might as well have been the Sahara Desert.

Charlie skated right, then made a sharp, quick turn left. He faked out Mitch, then Pudge. The two of them crashed into each other and went down.

Charlie grinned and looked up into the stands. The grin slipped off his face. No Dad.

Frost wobbled across the asphalt parking lot, his bottom ball sizzling and liquefying like a pat of butter in a hot frying pan. His boy was in there. And Frost had made a promise to him.

"Hot! Hot! Hot! Hot soup! Comin' through!" He felt himself shrinking with every step he took. Okay, he wasn't going to win any bathing suit contests with this body, but it was the only one he had these days, and he wanted to keep it.

Ooch! Owwch! He splattered his way across the lot. Getting shorter and smaller . . . But he wasn't going to give up. He'd disappointed Charlie too many times before.

Finally . . . ahhh! The bliss of the slushy patch of grass at the side of the stadium. He'd made it! All right, so he was a little on the short side now. But from here it was easier. Frost wobbled with new vigor, heading toward the side door of the rink.

Rory skated by Charlie at center ice. "Give up, Frost," he taunted.

Charlie didn't need to look up at the score clock. Last period, and it was still 1–zip. And no Dad. Maybe he *should* give up.

"Kick their butts, Charlie-boy!"

Dad! In the stadium. Charlie spun around on

the ice, trying to locate the voice. Not in the stands. He didn't see him. But he heard him again. "Go, Charlie!"

The voice was coming from under the bleachers. He'd made it! Charlie felt a jolt of energy.

Ignoring Rory, he skated down the ice. Natalie, her stick on the puck, saw him and winged him a perfect pass. Charlie didn't lose a second. Arms and wrists straight but relaxed. *BOOM!* His stick connected with the puck. He watched it sail. It was perfect! It was monstrous! The fans were on their feet. The puck flew at the Devils' goalie. It sizzled by him. Goal!

"Yessss!" Charlie did a little dance on his skates.

"Yessss! Yes, buddyyyy!" Frost yelled.

He'd done it! He'd scored! He'd made his first goal. And his father had actually watched it. Charlie pumped his arms in the air.

The crowd was going crazy. Even the old score-keeper was cheering. She rang up the goal. Tied at one apiece, with forty seconds left. This game wasn't over yet.

The ref threw the puck down. Charge! Rory got the puck and barreled down the open ice for the Mountaineers' net. Tuck, the goalie, cringed. C'mon, stand your ground, Charlie thought. Rory fired a blistering shot.

"Please, not in the face," Tuck moaned, but he dug in.

WHACK! The puck slammed into his mask. Tuck fell down on his butt — hard. But the puck bounced off his mask and out of the net. No score!

It was Dennis for the rebound. He roared up the ice with the rest of the Mountaineers. Charlie caught his pass and winged it to Natalie. Six seconds left. Natalie took a shot at the goal. It was clean. It was powerful.

Nice! Charlie thought, watching the puck soar. But the Devils' goalie blocked it with his big body. The puck dribbled in front of him on the ice.

"The Ricochet, Charlie, the Ricochet!" Frost called out.

Charlie checked out the position of the puck. And then the goalie's shiny-bladed skate. He knew what his father meant. He skated forward. Rory's arm came out. Charlie ducked under it and kept going. He reached with his stick and tipped the puck. *ZING!* It careened off the goalie's skate like a billiard ball and angled right into the net! Icy cool! He'd made another goal! And not just any goal — the *winning* goal!

Charlie looked up at the scoreboard and half expected it to be a dream. Devils: 1, Mountaineers: 2! The game buzzer sounded. Charlie was in seventh heaven. The fans raced onto the ice and circled around him. His teammates lifted him onto their shoulders! He was a hero!

15

Charlie waved good-bye to the last of his team-mates and ducked under the bleachers. Frost was waiting, a proud smile on his ball of a face.

"Killer game, Charlie-boy. You rocked," said his father.

Charlie's heart beat hard with excitement. "Yeah. It felt great."

"So, you're going to stick with this hockey thing?"

Charlie nodded. And then he saw it — the big puddle of water under his father. Frost was looking decidedly on the petite side. "Dad, you're crazy to come here," he said, suddenly panicked.

"Hey, a man's gotta keep his promises," his father said.

"Maybe we could cool you down on the ice," Charlie suggested. But the blaring of "Winter Wonderland" from the rink's speakers signaled the beginning of the free skate. A crowd of little kids shot onto the ice.

"I've got to get you someplace where it's really cold," Charlie said. The thrill of the hockey game was gone. Charlie didn't want to face what was happening. "I'm not losing you again," he said. But he was going to — if he didn't get help immediately.

He turned and started to run for the exit. "Charlie!" he heard his father call after him.

"I'll be back," Charlie yelled to him, without slowing down.

"Mom! Mom!" Charlie burst into the bank and raced to her window.

"Hey, no cutting," said one of the people in line.

"Mom, I need you to drive us somewhere right now!"

"Honey, I'm working," his mother said.

Panic beat in Charlie's chest. "You've *got* to!"

"What's wrong, sweetheart?"

"He's melting," Charlie blurted out.

"Who's melting?" his mother asked.

"The snowman! The snowman is melting!"

His mother's forehead creased. "Snowmen melt, Charlie. That's just the way it is."

"But if you drive us to —"

"— Charlie! I'm not driving you and your snowman anywhere!" his mother said sternly. "I don't know what's going on between you and that snowman, but it has to stop."

Behind Charlie, the people in line were beginning to grumble.

Charlie's breath came shallow and fast. That puddle around Dad was only going to get bigger. And Dad smaller. "You don't understand, Mom!" He felt his desperation swell. "He's Dad!" It just burst out of him. He couldn't hold it in any longer.

Complete silence fell over the room. All activity had stopped. Charlie felt every eye in the whole bank on him. Mom's mouth had dropped open practically to the floor. "He made me promise not to tell you. But Dad's the snowman. The snowman's Dad!"

"You father's gone, Charlie," his mother said, sadly but sternly.

"No. He's not. He's here. He came back as a snowman." But Charlie could see it was hopeless. Everyone in here thought he was cracked. Including Mom. He backed away.

"He died a year ago," his mother said, her voice sad and terribly worried, now. "You have to face it."

"Nooo!" Charlie cried. He turned and ran. He heard his mother calling after him, but he didn't stop. He fled down Main Street. He almost didn't see the man selling his last few Christmas trees from the Pine Top truck.

"It's now or never. My family's waiting to have Christmas!" the man said.

Charlie screeched to a stop. He looked at the man. And at his truck. And at the massive, white-capped mountains in the distance. His mood soared like a ski jumper.

He raced back to the ice stadium as fast as he could.

"Oh, my god!" Charlie wailed. He stared at the huge puddle of water where he'd last seen his father. Please, please, please . . . this couldn't be true.

He whirled around, looking for the snowman.

Just a trail of smaller puddles on the concrete floor. Don't let this happen, he thought. Not when salvation was just a truck ride away. Charlie followed the puddles out from under the bleachers and down the hall to the side exit.

He gasped. Dad! The wet heap of snow on the floor wore a hat and scarf.

"Charlie . . ." his father gurgled weakly. Clumps of slushy snow lay around him, melting fast.

Charlie dropped down to his father's side and began trying to repack the snow. "It's okay, Dad. I'm here," he said. But the snow wasn't sticking. Charlie was losing him. He packed harder. His arms shook. He couldn't catch his breath. What was he going to do? Who could help? He looked around, his thoughts spinning desperately, wildly.

His gaze landed on the dolly over by the exit — a metal cart with four wheels and a big handle to push it. Saved! Or at least not lost, yet.

Now Charlie was hot and dripping, too. He was using every muscle in his body to push the dolly down the street. Even melting, the snowman was heavy.

His father was spreading out like butter on warm

toast. He wasn't doing well at all. "I wish this thing had air-conditioning!" he cracked feebly.

There wasn't a second to lose. Charlie took a sharp turn into an alley. Out onto Pine Street and over to the green. Charlie didn't have a second to worry about the people stopping to gape at them — a boy pushing a snowman on a dolly.

Almost there. Past the church. Yes! Charlie spotted the Pine Top truck at the end of the block. Hallelujah! He got a burst of energy. But oh, no! The truck was pulling away. Charlie pushed the dolly into overdrive. His legs ached as he ran. His lungs burned. "No, wait!! Come back!!" he yelled.

He pushed the dolly right out into the middle of the street and raced after the truck. Behind him, he heard the blare of a horn and the screech of a car slamming on its brakes. Another screech. The sound of metal crunching against metal. An out-of-tune symphony of horns.

Charlie kept going. He didn't look back.

Frost wished he had the strength to tell Charlie to just let him melt in peace. The poor kid was exhausted. He pushed the dolly into the service station where the truck he was chasing had stopped for gas. From where he lay in a wet heap on the dolly, Frost could hear the pump whirring as it filled the truck's huge tank with diesel fuel.

"The driver's inside buying something!" Charlie told him, panting but sounding painfully hopeful. "Now's our chance." He pushed Frost toward the flatbed of the truck.

"Charlie . . ." Frost whispered. This whole thing was crazy. Maybe that was what happened when you had a dad who was kind of crazy himself.

The CB radio in the cab of the truck crackled. "And an all points bulletin has been issued for twelve-year-old Charles Frost, five-foot-one, blond hair, pushing a metal dolly with a snowman, three balls, two stick arms . . . well, you know what a snowman looks like. . . ."

Frost felt guilty. An APB. Gabby must have called the police. She was probably worried sick. And why? Because Frost had finally gone to see Charlie's game — only to cause more trouble than when he'd missed it.

But Charlie was lifting up the blue plastic tarp on the truck's flatbed, getting ready to try to load him on.

"Frost!" Huh? Was someone talking to him? A

big kid in baggy camouflage pants came out of the service station. But it was Charlie he was talking to. "You and me. Once and for all."

"Get out of my way, Rory," Charlie said.

"Make me."

"Look, I'll fight you any time you want," Charlie said. "Just not now! I'm asking you this one thing." Frost heard the desperation in his son's voice. Poor Charlie. And it was all his snowy — well, slushy — fault.

"I don't know who's stupider," the big kid said. "You or your snowman!" Frost saw him raise a clenched fist.

Was that mug calling his kid stupid? Frost felt a cold shot of anger. And it gave him just the last bit of strength he needed. "Stupider? Did you say stupider?" he asked.

The big kid looked around wide-eyed. "Who said that?"

"I did, you little baggy-pants snowpunk." Frost managed to push up from the dolly with his mittened hand. This Rory kid was staring at him, his mouth wide enough to drive the truck through.

"What . . . what the heck is it?" he asked, his voice trembling.

"Not what," said Charlie. "Who."

"Who the heck is it?"

"My dad," Charlie said.

Rory looked at Charlie. Then back at Frost. He broke into a wide grin. "I knew it! Mitch and Pudge said I was crazy! But I *knew* I saw him that day! You throw a mean snowball, dude . . . I couldn't believe it. . . ."

Frost sunk back down into a soupy heap. "Okay, okay," he said. "Don't have a meltdown."

"If I don't get him on that truck up to the mountains, I'm gonna lose him," Charlie told Rory urgently.

"He does look pretty bad," Rory said.

Frost didn't have enough left in him to protest that one.

"Please . . ." Charlie said, his voice wavering. "You know what it's like not to have a dad."

Frost shut his eyes. But he heard the big kid's answer. "It sucks. It sucks big-time."

There was a moment of silence. Then Frost felt himself being lifted onto the truck. "Don't do this," he whispered. "It's too dangerous."

But the boys hoisted him up and slid him under the tarp. "Sorry, Dad, but it's for your own good,"

Charlie said. And then he uttered a strangled little cry. "Oh, no . . . the driver."

"Under the truck," Rory said to Charlie.

Frost didn't hear anything for several long minutes. In the darkness under the tarp, his alarm spiraled. Was his boy all right? It would just kill him if anything happened to Charlie because of him.

And then he heard the truck's engine kick into gear. He felt the flatbed begin to vibrate. All of a sudden, he was moving. The truck was on the road. And Frost was leaving Charlie behind.

16

The rear axle of the flatbed passed just inches above Charlie's head. The huge wheels of the truck squealed and chattered. He held his breath, terror pounding in his heart. But the second the vehicle cleared him and Rory, they were on their feet in a flash, chasing after the back of the truck.

"Hey! What do you think you're doing?" Charlie felt a big, beefy hand grab his upper arm. The station attendant's muscles bulged out of his blue coveralls. He held Charlie in one hand, Rory in the other.

The truck — with Frost on it — rumbled away. Charlie strained to go after it. "Let me go! C'mon!" he shouted at the attendant.

"Yeah, why don't you pick on someone as dumb as you?" Rory said. He picked up one chunky snowboarding boot and brought it down hard on the attendant's sneaker.

"Why, you little . . ." The attendant let go of Charlie to give his full, I'm-gonna-throttle-you attention to Rory.

"Run, Charlie, run," Rory shouted to him.

Charlie took off after the truck, running with every ounce of energy he had. His arms pumped. His legs burned. But the truck was getting away from him. And so was his dad.

The sounds of classic rock 'n' roll oldies split the afternoon. The snowplow appeared from a side street, pulling across the road in front of the truck. The truck slowed down.

Charlie burned his very last smidgen of energy, like a world-class athlete at the finish line. He sprinted up to the back of the truck and leaped. He caught onto the iron bar across the back of the flatbed. The snowplow lumbered across the street and out of the way. The truck sped up. Charlie pulled himself up and slid under the tarp.

*　　*　　*

Frost yawned, stretched, and opened his eyes. The first thing he saw was his son's heartbreakingly sweet face.

"It's getting cold, Dad. Are you feeling better?" Charlie asked, his voice filled with concern.

Frost sat up. Charlie had pushed off the tarp. He could see the deep purple silhouettes of the mountains on either side of the road. The truck climbed a steep, winding peak. He smiled. "This is short-sleeve weather for me," he said. He noticed that Charlie's lips were quivering. "But not for you. We've got to get you someplace warm."

"We're there," Charlie answered stoically. "You've been out for a long time."

The truck pulled over the crest, took a brief downhill, and started chugging back up again. At the bottom of the long, gentle slope on one side of the road, a pristine field of snow glistened. White-topped pine trees bordered the field. Frost recognized this stretch. He and Charlie had thrown snowballs in that field in the winter.

He felt Charlie nudge him. "You ready? On three," Charlie said, getting into a crouch by the side of the flatbed.

"I've got you, buddy," Frost told him. He got into position next to his son. "One . . ."

"Two . . ." said Charlie.

"Three!" they both yelled. They leaped from the truck. Frost got his stick arms around Charlie and cushioned his fall. Holding his son close to him, they rolled down the hill. As he let go, Charlie clambered to his feet. Frost took a few more rolls in the cold, powdery snow. He lolled on his back like Chester did in the grass.

"Fresh powder. My favorite." He let out an icicle-clear, crisp laugh. He scooped up the snow by the mittenful, packing it onto himself and gaining back everything that had melted away.

"Come on, Dad! Follow me!" Charlie shouted. He plowed through the deep snow.

Frost followed, waddling and rolling.

The glass shattered with a tinkle like cracked ice as Frost punched his mitten through the pane in the cabin door. He reached inside with one long stick arm and turned the inside handle. The door opened in a spray of snow. Frost staggered in, carrying Charlie on his back.

"We're here, Dad. . . . We made it. . . ." Charlie said, his voice soft with contentment and sleepiness.

"Yes, Charlie, we made it." Frost carried his son into the comfortable, homey little log cabin and gently laid him down on the sofa. He took the quilt folded neatly over the back and spread it over Charlie carefully.

Charlie's blue eyes fluttered closed. Frost studied his long, dark blond lashes, his soft, full mouth, the curve of his cheeks. If snowmen had hearts, his was definitely breaking. When was the last time he'd stopped and just watched his boy while he was sleeping? When was the last time he'd taken a moment to do nothing but be with him?

"I was so busy. . . ." Frost whispered. "Tryin' to make my mark on the world . . ." Lightly, he brushed a loose lock of silky hair from Charlie's brow. "You *are* my mark on the world." He bent toward Charlie and kissed his forehead softly.

Charlie opened his eyes sleepily. "That night you came back," he said. "It was 'cause I played your harmonica. I wished it. I wished for you to be here for Christmas."

Frost felt the tears welling up and spilling over. "Thanks, Charlie. Thanks for giving me a second chance to be your dad."

Frost got a crackling fire going while Charlie slept peacefully. There was only one more thing Frost had to do. He went over to the old red rotary phone and dialed his home number.

Gabby picked it up in the middle of the first ring. "Hello? Hello?"

"Gabby . . ."

"Who is this?" Gabby asked frantically. "Did you find him?"

Frost glanced at Charlie's peaceful face. "The little guy's sleeping. He's had one heck of a day."

"Is he all right?" Gabby asked.

"He scored his first goal. You should have seen him. He was really something. . . ."

"Who is this? Where's Charlie?" Gabby's words came out in a rush.

"He's at the cabin at Pine Top. Why don't you come get him? . . ."

There was stark silence at the other end of the line. Then Gabby's voice came through the telephone in a shaky whisper. "Jack?"

Frost stared at the receiver. Gently, he hung it back up. Now he knew he had a broken heart.

He got up and put one more log on the fire. He took a long look at Charlie. Then he let himself out of the cabin and back into the snow.

Charlie raced out of the cabin. The early rays of morning light fell across the white wilderness. The air was bitingly cold but fresh. His father stood in front of the little house like — well, like a snowman. But he was here! Here in Pine Top with Charlie for Christmas. Okay, so he was a year late, but Dad was never on time.

"Merry Christmas, Dad!" Charlie ran up to him, his feet sinking into the snow.

"Merry Christmas, Charlie-boy." He showered his son with a smile loving and bright enough to melt him. But there was something sad about it, too. "Charlie . . ." his father said gently.

Charlie heard a motor and he whirled around. The Frosts' Jeep was struggling up the long, snow-covered dirt road leading to the cabin. Mom!

"You know it's time to say good-bye," Dad finished.

Charlie whirled back around. His heart skipped

a beat. Good-bye?! "No!" Every cell in his body rebelled against the idea. "I won't let you go!"

"You have to, Charlie. It's time to get on with your life," his father said.

"It'll get cold again, you'll see!" Charlie reasoned. "Winter's just barely started!"

"And what happens when spring comes along? What happens come summer?"

Charlie was stuck for a second. "We'll . . . we'll go to South America! When it's summer here, it's winter there!"

"Smart kid!" His father gave an impressed nod.

"Take me with you," Charlie pleaded.

"What about Mom? She needs you, Charlie."

Charlie looked down the road. The Jeep was stuck in a deep snowdrift. The driver's door opened. Mom jumped out. "Charlie!" She struggled toward him.

"We've been lucky to have this time together," Charlie's father said.

Charlie turned back to him. He could keep arguing with Dad, but he knew he was right. Snowmen didn't last forever. Not even this one. He blinked furiously against the tears. "Will I ever see you again?"

Dad smiled a soft, powder-snow smile. "As long as you hold someone in your heart, you'll never lose them. You let me back into yours, Charlie. I'll always be there for you." He took off his burgundy scarf and wrapped it around Charlie's neck. "Thank you, Charlie. No one can ever take me away from you. And if someone is dumb enough to try, just blow on that harmonica." He reached up for his hat and plopped it on Charlie's head.

Charlie felt the light dusting of snow on the scarf melt like tears on the warmth of his skin. "I love you, Dad," he whispered softly.

"I love you, too, Charlie," his father whispered back.

And then they were hugging — a powerful, snowy hug. Charlie held on for dear life.

"Now let me go, Charlie," his father said gently. "Let me go." He eased his way out of Charlie's grasp.

The tears were rolling freely down Charlie's face now, hot in the cold air. He let his arms drop to his sides. His father took a wobbling step back from him. Charlie felt the wind pick up. The pine trees around the house danced crazily, releasing a fine shower of snow into the air. Wisps of snow began to swirl around his father.

"Oh, Charlie! Thank God!" Gabby called out. Charlie turned to her. She ran the final steps to him, her arms outstretched. And then her gaze landed on the snowman and she froze in her tracks. Charlie turned back.

The wind began to circle around the snowman with more and more force. It seemed to peel away a layer of his snow as it spun, whirling it into a white tornado around him. And then another layer. The wind whipped faster and faster.

Charlie stared harder. There was something inside the snowman. Some kind of glowing form. Layer after layer of snow was shed. No, he wasn't imagining it. It was a human form. Shimmering, glistening, all crystalline light. His father! Dad! The way he once was. Standing in the center of a spinning vortex of snow.

"Jack! I love you," Gabby cried.

"I love you, too." Tears were streaming down his father's luminous face. But through his tears, he smiled at Gabby. Then at Charlie. "We had us a time, didn't we, Charlie-boy?" He was starting to dissolve, fading into the bright morning.

"Yeah, Dad, we sure did," answered Charlie.

And then he was gone. The whirlwind stopped. The snowflakes floated into the sky or fluttered to the ground.

"Good-bye," Charlie whispered. And then he and his mom were in each other's arms.

Charlie whacked the puck into the target on his garage. Score! Inside, Mac was banging out a cool, rocking, bluesy version of "Frosty the Snowman." The front door opened and Chester scampered out of the house. Mom stuck her head out and gave Charlie a little wave before disappearing back inside.

The weather had turned colder again, just as Charlie had predicted. Everyone else on his block was inside, staying warm and playing with their new Christmas presents. But Charlie felt good out in the new snow. Fresh powder. Dad's favorite.

He watched as Chester trotted across the street to Natalie's house and barked at the snowman in her front yard. He lifted his leg and let out a yellow stream on it.

Charlie laughed and shook his head. He turned back to his driveway practice arena and took another shot at the bulls'-eye. *BOOM!* A snowball hit him squarely in the back. He spun around. But he was nothing, nobody on the street in one direction or the other.

Nothing but snowmen, standing silent guard on every snowy lawn.